Samuel French Acting Editi

Mother o

By
Evan Placey

ıl SAMUEL FRENCH lı

SAMUELFRENCH.COM   SAMUELFRENCH.CO.UK

ISBN 978-0-573-70101-6

www.SamuelFrench.com
www.SamuelFrench.co.uk

FOR PRODUCTION ENQUIRIES

UNITED STATES AND CANADA
Info@SamuelFrench.com
1-866-598-8449

UNITED KINGDOM AND EUROPE
Plays@SamuelFrench.co.uk
020-7255-4302

Each title is subject to availability from Samuel French, depending upon country of performance. Please be aware that MOTHER OF HIM may not be licensed by Samuel French in your territory. Professional and amateur producers should contact the nearest Samuel French office or licensing partner to verify availability.

For enquiries relating to UK professional rights; amateur rights outside of the UK and US and rights in all other media including motion picture and television please contact The Agency (London) Ltd, 24, Pottery Lane, London, W11 4LZ

MUSIC USE NOTE

Licensees are solely responsible for obtaining formal written permission from copyright owners to use copyrighted music in the performance of this play and are strongly cautioned to do so. If no such permission is obtained by the licensee, then the licensee must use only original music that the licensee owns and controls. Licensees are solely responsible and liable for all music clearances and shall indemnify the copyright owners of the play(s) and their licensing agent, Samuel French, against any costs, expenses, losses and liabilities arising from the use of music by licensees. Please contact the appropriate music licensing authority in your territory for the rights to any incidental music.

IMPORTANT BILLING AND CREDIT REQUIREMENTS

If you have obtained performance rights to this title, please refer to your licensing agreement for important billing and credit requirements.

MOTHER OF HIM had its world premiere at the Courtyard Theatre in London, UK in June, 2010. The production was directed by Guy Retallack, and the Assistant Director was Antje Timmerman. The Producer was June Abbott. Lighting design was by Giuliano Bocca, with sound design by Matt Eaton. The Fight Director was Marcello Marascalchi, and the Set Designer was John Bell. The Stage Manager was David Palmer. The cast was as follows:

BRENDA KAPOWITZ .... Madeleine Potter

JASON KAPOWITZ ....William Byrne/Gideon Leibowitz

MATTHEW KAPOWITZ............................Tom Golding

ROBERT ROSENBERG ....Dale Rapley

JESSICA.....................................Jennifer Thompson

STEVEN .... Chris Gilling

TESS ....
....Sarah Cherkowey

MOTHER OF HIM opened at Park Theatre, London on September 18, 2019. The cast was as follows:

BRENDA KAPOWITZ .... Tracy-Ann Oberman

JASON KAPOWITZ .... Matt Goldberg/Hari Aggarwal

MATTHEW KAPOWITZ .... Scott Folan

ROBERT ROSENBERG .... Simon Hepworth

JESSICA/TESS .... Anjelica Serra

STEVEN .... Neil Sheffield

DIRECTED BY .... Max Linsday

COSTUME SUPERVISOR .... Jessica Richardson-Smith

PRODUCTION MANAGERS .... Tom Nickson and Luis Henson

VOICE AND ACCENT COACH. .... Edda Sharpe

FIGHT DIRECTOR .... Kenan Ali

CASTING DIRECTOR. .... Emma Garrett

CAST

HARI AGGARWAL - Jason Kapowitz
Hari is currently training at the Italia Conti Academy Of Theatre Arts.

Previous credits include: Young Macduff *Macbeth* (RSC); *Wall Street Banker*, *We Can Do Better* Music Video with Matt Simons/Forever Pictures

Hari is thrilled to be joining the cast of *Mother of Him* at Park Theatre.

SCOTT FOLAN - Matthew Kapowitz
Scott most recently appeared as Matt in Chichester Festival Theatre's *This is my Family,* written by Tim Firth.

Scott began his professional career in 2012 in Debbie Isitt's feature film *Nativity 2: Danger in the Manger*. He then went on to appear in The National Theatre's *Damned By Despair* the following year. Since then Scott has starred in the 2015 Comedy Central sitcom *Brotherhood*, CBBC's *Dixi4* and Gurinder Chadha's 2019 feature film *Blinded By The Light*.

Other theatre includes: *Sunday In The Park With George* (National Youth Music Theatre at The Other Palace); *Dre*, *The Lost Ones* and Moritz' Father in *Spring Awakening* (Leicester Curve) directed by Nikolai Foster.

Other Television and Film includes: *Breathless* (ITV); Bully in EnyPictures' *Cafe Afrik* (pilot) and *Outside Bet* – short film.

Scott is also an emerging singer-songwriter who writes in a Pop-Folk style. His music can be found on all major music platforms including Spotify and Apple Music or from his social media platforms under the tag @scott_folan

MATT GOLDBERG - Jason Kapowitz
Matt is twelve years old, the youngest of four brothers and attends University College School in Hampstead. Whilst attending vocational classes at the Sylvia Young Theatre School he was offered representation by the schools agency and his professional work includes: Young Orestes in *Oresteia* (Trafalgar Studios); Leonard in *At Arms Length* a short film directed by Max Weilland. Various radio and TV commercials and also voiced the character Fenuku in the video game *Aegyptus*.

Matt plays piano and guitar and enjoys kickboxing and computer coding. He is thrilled to be joining the cast of *Mother of Him* at Park Theatre

SIMON HEPWORTH – Robert Rosenberg
Simon was born in Blackpool and trained at LAMDA, winning the St Philip's Trophy.

Theatre includes: *Absolute Hell* (Royal National Theatre); *Antony & Cleopatra* (Chichester Festival Theatre); *The Lion in Winter* (Theatre Royal Haymarket); *King Lear* (Guildford Shakespeare Company); *Joe & I* (King's Head); *The Rivals* (Compass Theatre Company); *A Midsummer Night's Dream, Macbeth* (Arundel Festival and tour); *Twelfth Night* (Bristol Old Vic); *The Winter's Tale, The Glass Menagerie, The Deep Blue Sea* (Royal & Derngate, Northampton); *John Cleese's Bang Bang, Romeo and Juliet, Burn This, Tartuffe, My Cousin Rachel,* (Mercury Theatre, Colchester); *Mario and the Magician* (Almeida); the *Agatha Christie Theatre Festival 2001* (Palace, Westcliff); *The Best Man, Blood Brothers, The Hollow* (BKL UK tours).

Television includes: *Endeavour, Fearless, EastEnders, Foyle's War, Casualty, Law And Order UK, Emmerdale, Coronation Street, Doctors,* Lynda la Plante's *Trial and Retribution, Wire in the Blood, Wallis and Edward, Inspector Morse – The Remorseful Day, Doctors, The Royal, The Bill, Bliss, Bodyguards, Departures,* Ruth Rendell's *Thornapple* and *The Young Indiana Jones Chronicles* (Lucasfilm).

Film includes: *Walking With The Enemy, Sink, Love's Kitchen, 47 Cleveland, The Holly Kane Experiment, Tezz and The Walker,* directed by Paul Schrader.

TRACY-ANN OBERMAN – Brenda Kapowitz
Theatre includes: *Party Time/Celebration* (Harold Pinter Theatre); *Pack of Lies* (Menier Chocolate Factory); *Present Laughter; Fiddler On The Roof* and *Saturday, Sunday... & Monday* (Chichester Festival Theatre); *Loot and Two* (Chichester Minerva Theatre and Vaudeville Theatre); *Stepping Out* (Vaudeville Theatre and UK Tour); *McQueen* (St James Theatre and Theatre Royal Haymarket); *Godchild, Old Money* and *On The Rocks* (Hampstead Theatre); *Earthquakes in London* (National Theatre); *Absurd Person Singular* (Leicester Curve Theatre); *Boeing Boeing* (Comedy Theatre); *The Oak Tree* and *School Play* (Soho Theatre); *Edmond* and *Waiting for Leftie* (National Theatre); *Hello Goodbye* (Southwark Playhouse); *A Call In The Night* (West Yorkshire Playhouse); *A Christmas Carol, The Changeling, Tamburlaine, The Beggers Opera, A Jovial Crew* and *Macbeth* (RSC).

Television includes: *Code 404* (Kudos); *Dad's Army* (UKTV); *Afterlife* (Netflix); *Zapped, Hoff The Record* (Dave); *Friday Night Dinner* Series 1-5 (BigTalk); *Toast of London* Series 1-3 (Objective); *Siblings* (Bwark Productions); *Tracey Breaks The News, Doctor Who, Father Brown, New Tricks, Crims, The Way It Is, Happiness, 15 Stories High, Harringham Harker, Mistresses, Robin Hood, Summerhill, Sorted, Sadie Jones, Tracey*

Beaker Returns, Best of Men, EastEnders (BBC); *Comedy Playhouse, Marion and Geoff* (BBC/Baby Cow); *The Last Detective, Murder in Suburbia, Where The Heart Is* (ITV); *The Cow* (C4); *Filth* (C4/Angel Eye); *Bob Martin* (Granada); *M.I. High* (Kudos); *Monroe* (Mammoth / ITV); *Waterloo Road* (Shed Productions); *Big Train* (Talkback).

Film includes: *Where's Anne Frank, The Casanova Variations, Hector & The Search for Happiness, The Funeral, Filth, Wall, Girl Number 9, The Infidel, The Early Days, Supertex, Killing Time* and *Hope Machine*.

ANJELICA SERRA – Jessica/Tess
Theatre includes: *The Suppliant Women, And Yet It Moves* and *The American Dream 2.0* (Young Vic) and *Connections* (Theatre503).

Short Film includes: *Dormitory* (Dir. Lab Ky Mo); *Michelle* (Dir. Ben Drew)

Anjelica is a British Filipino actor hailing from London and is proud to be making her Park Theatre debut.

NEIL SHEFFIELD – Steven
Theatre includes: *Tracing Grace* (West Yorkshire Playhouse); *Bud* (Arts Theatre); *Cross* (The Vaults); *How To Think The Unthinkable* (Unicorn Theatre); *Less Than Kind* (UK Tour); *Therese Raquin* (Riverside Studios), *The Wind in the Willows* (West End & UK Tour); *The Trials of Brendan Behan* (Irish Centre); *Golden Boy* (West Yorkshire Playhouse & UK Tour); *Anna Christie* (Riverside Studios); *The Cockroach Dialogues* (Theatre503); *The Marriage* (The Lyric, Belfast); *The City Club* (The Pleasance); *A Christmas Tale* (Bristol Old Vic); *Dracula* (Hackney Empire); *The Seagull* (Moscow Arts Theatre) and *Macbeth* (Union Theatre & Riverside Studios).

Television includes: *Catch Me If You Can, Reality Check, The Demon Headmaster*.

Film incudes: *Alive, The Projectionist, Witchcraft X, The Retreat* and *Cash in Hand*.

CREATIVES

EVAN PLACEY - WRITER

Evan is a Canadian-British playwright and screenwriter who grew up in Toronto and now lives in London. His work for adults and young audiences has been produced internationally and translated into multiple languages. His debut play *Mother of Him* won the King's Cross Award for New Writing, Canada's RBC National Playwriting Competition (Tarragon), and the Samuel French Canadian Play Contest, and was shortlisted for the Meyer Whitworth Award and the Rod Hall Memorial Award. It was adapted for BBC Radio 3. Evan won the Brian Way Award for *Holloway Jones* (Synergy Theatre/Unicorn), while *Girls Like That* (Birmingham REP/Plymouth Drum/West Yorkshire Playhouse & Synergy/Unicorn) won the Writers' Guild Award for Best Play for Young Audiences, the Scenic Youth Prize and the Orpheon Bibliotheque Prize for Contemporary Theatre for Young Audiences in France and the Jugend Theatre Preis Baden-Wurttemberg in Germany. *Scarberia* (Young People's Theatre, Toronto) was nominated for five Dora Awards in Canada.

Other plays include: *Consensual* (NYT/West End); *Jekyll & Hyde* (NYT/West End & Birmingham REP); *Orange Polar Bear* (Birmingham REP/National Theatre Company of Korea); *Keepy Uppy* (tutti frutti/UK tour); *Consensual* (NYT/West End); *Pronoun* (National Theatre); *WiLd!* (tutti/fruttiUK tour); *Little Criminals* (Polka/Plymouth Drum/York Theatre Royal); *How Was It For You?* (Unicorn) and *Banana Boys* (Hampstead). Evan is Creative Writing Fellow at the University of Southampton, and also teaches playwriting for the National Theatre, Arvon, and in prisons.

MAX LINDSAY - DIRECTOR

Director credits include: *Ripped* (Underbelly, Edinburgh); *Angry* (Southwark Playhouse); *Foreign Goods 2* and *Broken Gargoyles* (Theatre503); *Consensual, The Odyssey, Girls Like That, Henry IV, His Dark Materials, The Laramie Project Circle, The Wardrobe, Feathers in the Snow, Great Expectations, The Three Musketeers* and *Cymbeline* (Nuffield Theatre); *Someone to Blame* (Kings Head Theatre/Nuffield Theatre); *Jimmy Jimmy* (Omnibus Clapham); *The Best Christmas Present* (The Playing Field); *The Voyage of Lost Dreams* (SS Shieldhall).

Associate and Assistant Director credits include: *Cargo* (regional tour); *We Are Here* (National Theatre); as Assistant Director: *Me and My Girl* and *The Midnight Gang* (Chichester Festival Theatre); *Snow White and the Seven Dwarves* (Theatre Royal Plymouth); *Cargo* (Arcola London); *The Nutcracker* (Nuffield Theatre). Max was Resident Assistant Director at Chichester Festival Theatre for Festival 2018 where he assisted Tinuke Craig, Dale Rooks and Daniel Evans. He was previously at Nuffield Southampton Theatres. He trained at East 15.

LEE NEWBY - SET AND COSTUME DESIGNER

Credits include: *The Life I Lead* (Wyndham's Theatre / UK Tour);
Musik, Cruel Intentions, The Crown Dual (Edinburgh Festival 2019);
The View Upstairs (Soho Theatre); *Vienna 1934 – Munich 1938*
(Ustinov Studio, Bath Theatre Royal); *Prayer For Wings* (Volcano
Theatre, Swansea); *Whodunnit [Unrehearsed], Gently Down the
Stream* (Park Theatre); *Mythic* (Charing Cross Theatre); *Abigail's
Party, Abi* (Queen's Theatre Hornchurch/Derby Theatre); *Homos, Or
Everyone in America* (Finborough Theatre); *Romeo and Juliet, Richard
III* (Shakespeare's Rose Theatre, York); *Labour of Love* (Noel Coward
Theatre); *The Importance of Being Earnest* (Theatr Clwyd); *Lunch,
The Bow of Ulysses* (Trafalgar Studios 2); *The Tempest, Deathwatch,
Ignis* (Print Room); *Floyd Collins* (Wilton's Music Hall); *Stay Awake
Jake* (The Vault Festival); *First Lady Suite* (Mountview); *Grand Hotel,
Dogfight* (Southwark Playhouse); *Violet, Spend Spend Spend* (LSMT).
Associate design credits include: *Lazarus* (DeLaMar Theatre,
Amsterdam / King's Cross Theatre); *Vanya and Sonia and Masha and
Spike* (Ustinov Studio, Bath Theatre Royal); *Lady Day at Emerson's Bar
and Grill* (Wyndham's Theatre); *Romeo and Juliet* (Garrick Theatre);
*Photograph 51, Henry V, A Midsummer Night's Dream, The Cripple
of Inishmaan, Peter and Alice, Privates on Parade* (Noel Coward
Theatre); *A Damsel in Distress* (Chichester); *Carousel* (Lyric Opera of
Chicago/Houston Grand Opera); *Wolf Hall: Parts 1 & 2* (RSC/Aldwych/
Broadway); *Macbeth* (Manchester International Festival/New York);
Hughie, Cat on a Hot Tin Roof (Broadway).

ALI HUNTER - LIGHTING DESIGNER

Lighting Design Credits: *For Services Rendered, The Play About my
Dad, Woman before a Glass*; (Jermyn Street), *Cash Cow* (Hampstead);
Muckers (The Egg, Conde Duque, Oxford Playhouse); *Soft Animals*
(Soho); *Don't Forget the Birds, Rattlesnake* (Open Clasp); *I know not
these my hands, Happy Fathers' Day, Sugarman* and *All in Minor* (The
Place); *Clear White Light* (Live Theatre Newcastle); *Treemonisha,
The Boatswain's Mate* (Arcola); *Isaac Came Home from the Mountain,
Cinderella and the Beanstalk* (Theatre 503); *Gracie, The Biograph Girl*
(Finborough); *Tenderly* (New Wimbledon Studio); *Katzenmusik* (Royal
Court); *Foreign Body* (Southbank Centre for WOW).

As Associate Lighting Designer: *Hot Mess for Candoco Dance, The Half
God of Rainfall* (Birmingham Rep and Kiln).

Ali is the Young Associate Lighting Designer for Matthew Bourne's
Romeo and Juliet.

FERGUS O'HARE - SOUND DESIGNER

Credits include over 300 productions throughout the UK, Europe and
the US.

For Park Theatre *Daytona.*

Recent work includes: *Musik* (Assembly/Leicester SquareTheatre);
Apollo 11 (Rose Bowl L.A.); *Shadowlands* (CFT); *Agnes Colander*
(Jermyn Street Theatre); *A Christmas Carol* (RSC).

PRODUCERS

JACOB THOMAS
Jacob Thomas is an independent producer who, whilst establishing
Jacob Thomas Productions, currently works as the Production Assistant
at Jonathan Church Productions and as the Associate Producer at
Nouveau Riche.

Prior to this he had worked within the producing team at Chichester
Festival Theatre since November 2017, working across shows such as
Forty Years On and *King Lear*, as well as the entire of the 2018 season.

Previous independent productions include: *Poisoned Beds* (South East
coastal tour); *Who Cares* (Festival of Chichester). He has also worked
on CFT productions such as: *Forty Years On* (2017); *Flowers For Mrs
Harris* and *The Midnight Gang* (2018 - Festival Theatre, Chichester).
King Lear (2017), *The Country Wife*, *The Meeting* and *The Watsons*
(2018 - Minerva Theatre, Chichester).

OLIVER MACKWOOD LTD
Prior to establishing Oliver Mackwood Productions, Oliver worked
under the guidance of Sir Cameron Mackintosh, in-house at Chichester
Festival Theatre, and as an Associate Producer at Jonathan Church
Productions.

Oliver is a member of the Society of London Theatre and has produced
work in the West End, Internationally, and around the UK.

For Oliver Mackwood Productions: *Pressure* (Ambassadors Theatre,
West End); *In the Willows* (UK Tour); *Madame Rubinstein*, *What
Shadows*, *Dinner with Friends* (Park Theatre); *Sand in the Sandwiches*
(Theatre Royal Haymarket, West End and UK Tour); *Vixen* (UK, China,
Italy).

For Jonathan Church Productions, *Singin' In the Rain* (Japan); *Love's
Labour's Lost*; *Much Ado About Nothing* (West End); *Frozen* (West End),
Misty (West End); *The Life I Lead* (UK Tour); *This House* (UK Tour).

For Chichester Festival Theatre, *Guys & Dolls*, *Gypsy*, *The Rehearsal*,
Mack & Mabel, *Frankie & Johnny*, *Way Upstream*, *Running Wild*.

www.olivermackwood.com

Oliver Mackwood Ltd has produced five shows at Park Theatre
including: *What Shadows* (UK Tour); *Madame Rubenstein*, *Dinner
With Friends*, and *Pressure* (Park Theatre and West End).

THANKS

KD Builders – Set
White Light – Hire of Lighting Equipment
Stage Sound Services – Hire of Sound Equipment
JHI – Marketing
EHPR – PR
Target Live – Trailer
Park Theatre – Rehearsal Space
Kate Condon – Props Sourcing
Studio Doug – Poster Image and Artworking
Bronwen Sharpe – Poster, Rehearsal and Production Photography
Chichester Festival Theatre – Audition Space

PLAYWRIGHT'S ACKNOWLEDGMENTS

Mother of Him would not have been possible were it not for the
generous support, encouragement and insight of many people along the
way – too many to name here. I would, however, especially like to thank:
Max Lindsay, Jacob Thomas, Tracy-Ann Oberman, the cast, crew, and
staff at the Park Theatre and Oliver Mackwood Productions; the panel
of the King's Cross Award; ATC, The Finborough Theatre, The Tarragon
Theatre, and the Royal Court Young Writers' Programme, who all
contributed to various stages in the play's development; Jane Fallowfield
and Tessa Walker; Ben Rix and Little Brother Productions; Beit Lessin
Theatre; Madeleine Potter; Tanya Tillett and the Agency; my family,
Danny and K.

STAGE ONE

The producers of *Mother of Him* wish to acknowledge financial support from Stage One, a registered charity that invests in new commercial productions. Stage One supports new UK theatre producers and productions, and is committed to securing the future of commercial theatre through educational and investment schemes. Stage One would like to thank the Society of London Theatre and theatre producers and owners who voluntarily contribute to the levy – all of which support the Investment Scheme. For further information please visit www.stageone.uk.com, call 020 7557 6737 or follow us on Twitter @stageonenewprod

Stage One is the operating name of the Theatre Investment Fund Ltd, a registered charity no.271349

About Park Theatre

Park Theatre was founded by Artistic Director, Jez Bond and Associate Artistic Director, Melli Marie. The building opened in May 2013 and, with eight West End transfers, two National Theatre transfers and 25 national tours in its first six years, quickly garnered a reputation as a key player in the London theatrical scene. Park Theatre has received four Olivier nominations, won Offie Awards for Best New Play, Best Set Design and Best Foodie Experience, and won The Stage's Fringe Theatre of the Year in 2015.

Park Theatre is an inviting and accessible venue, delivering work of exceptional calibre in the heart of Finsbury Park. We work with writers, directors and designers of the highest quality to present compelling, exciting and beautifully told stories across our two intimate spaces.

Our programme encompasses a broad range of work from classics to revivals with a healthy dose of new writing, producing in-house as well as working in partnership with emerging and established producers. We strive to play our part within the UK's theatre ecology by offering mentoring, support and opportunities to artists and producers within a professional theatre-making environment.

Our Creative Learning strategy seeks to widen the number and range of people who participate in theatre, and provides opportunities for those with little or no prior contact with the arts.

In everything we do we aim to be warm and inclusive; a safe, welcoming and wonderful space in which to work, create and visit.

★★★★★ **"A five-star neighbourhood theatre." Independent**

As a registered charity [number 1137223] with no public subsidy, we rely on the kind support of our donors and volunteers. To find out how you can get involved visit parktheatre.co.uk

For Park Theatre

Artistic Director | Jez Bond
Executive Director | Rachael Williams
Associate Artistic Director | Melli Marie
Development Director | Dorcas Morgan
Sales & Marketing Director | Dawn James
Marketing Manager | Liam McLaughlin
Sales Manager | Julia Yelland
Finance Manager | Elaine Lavelle
Development & Production Assistant | Daniel Cooper
Technical and Buildings Manager | Sacha Queiroz
Deputy Technical and Buildings Manager | Neal Gray
Administrator | Melissa Bonnelame
Community Engagement Manager | Nina Graveney-Edwards
Access Coordinator | Sarah Howard
Venue & Volunteer Manager | Barry Card
Deputy Venue & Volunteer Manager | Michael Peavoy
Duty Venue Managers | Abigail Acons-Grocock, Natasha Green, Shaun Joynson
Head of Food and Beverage | Oli Mortimer
Cafe Bar Team | Grace Boateng, Gemma Barnet,
Florence Blackmore, James Bradwell, Ewan Brand,
Amy Conway, Adam Harding Kheir, Sebastian Harker, Kerry Hunt,
Matt Littleson, Jack Mosedale, Libby Nash, Josh Oakes Rodgers,
Ryan Peek, Alice Pegram, Maisie Saidgrove, Mitch Snell and
Holly Adomah Thompson
Senior Box Office Supervisor | Natasha Green
Box Office Supervisors | Greg Barnes and Jack Mosedale

Public Relations | Nick Pearce and Julie Holman for Target Live

President | Jeremy Bond

Ambassadors
David Horovitch
Celia Imrie
Sean Mathias
Tanya Moodie
Hattie Morahan
Tamzin Outhwaite
Meera Syal

Associate Artist
Mark Cameron

With thanks to all of our supporters, donors and volunteers.

SETTING

Toronto, Ontario, Canada. It's cold. Snowy.

The play takes place solely in the Kapowitz house, but the presence of what is going on outside the home should always be felt, though it is important we never see any of the photographers/press outside – only their voices and the flashes of cameras.

It should feel as though the house is getting smaller, closing in on them, as the play goes on.

Some of the sounds for transitions between scenes are included. Where it is not, it is at the discretion of the director. Though it should help us in hearing/feeling the chaos going on outside the house.

TIME

December, 1998.

AUTHOR'S NOTES

Slashes (/) denote the point of interruption, and the dialogue which interrupts it.
Ellipses (...) are an unfinished thought or a search for words.
Dashes (–) are lines that are cut off, sometimes by one's own interrupting thought. These are not pauses or beats.

Though this play was inspired by true events, the characters and story are all fictional. Any resemblance to persons living or dead is purely coincidental.

CHARACTERS

BRENDA KAPOWITZ

JASON KAPOWITZ – 8, Brenda's son

MATTHEW KAPOWITZ – 17, Brenda's son

ROBERT ROSENBERG – Matthew's lawyer and Brenda's friend

JESSICA – 16, Matthew's girlfriend

STEVEN – Brenda's ex-husband

TESS – Brenda's cleaning lady. Filipino

ACT 1

Scene One
Wednesday

(Kitchen. Morning.

A side entrance door in the kitchen leads to the street. Another door leads to the living room/rest of the house.

The kitchen is clean, immaculate...so immaculate that there is something off about it. The blinds are closed.

A pile of newspapers sits on the counter.

BRENDA *is sitting at the kitchen table, in a bathrobe...hair done up, no make-up yet. She holds one of the newspapers, staring at it. Behind her, breakfast is cooking on the stove.*

Breakfast begins to burn.)

BRENDA. Shit.

(**JASON** *enters playing a PSP [portable video game] and sits down at the table. He notices the open newspaper, goes to pick it up, but* **BRENDA** *grabs it away.)*

Why aren't you dressed? Jason?

JASON. I made it to level eight.

BRENDA. Honey, you need to get dressed. You're going to be late. Jason?

JASON. I don't want to go to school.

BRENDA. Go get dressed, sweetie.

JASON. Mom, I don't want to go to school today.

7

BRENDA. Jason –

JASON. I want to stay home with Matthew.

(pause)

BRENDA. Get dressed.

JASON. I really don't want to go, Mom.

BRENDA. I don't really want to go to work but I have to or else we wouldn't –

JASON. Yeah but –

BRENDA. And I don't want to be cooking your breakfast and making your lunch but I have to, because –

JASON. Because it's good for me.

BRENDA. Because I'm your mom. And moms have to make sure their kids eat. And eight year-old boys have to go to school.

*(**BRENDA** puts two plates of breakfast on the table. And a glass of orange juice.)*

Where are you going?

JASON. To get dressed.

BRENDA. Eat first, before it gets cold.

JASON. Is there any ketchup?

BRENDA. Sorry.

JASON. I thought I saw some in the fridge.

BRENDA. There isn't. Anyway it's full of sugar.

*(The phone starts to ring. **BRENDA** doesn't even look up.)*

JASON. Is Matthew coming down? *(pause)* Mom?

BRENDA. I don't know.

JASON. Do you want me to get him?

BRENDA. He'll come down when he's ready.

JASON. His food's getting cold.

*(**JASON** picks up his video game and starts to play.)*

BRENDA. Eat.

(BRENDA's Nokia rings. She checks the number, then exits while answering the phone.)

(JASON stands up, goes to the fridge. Still playing his game as he does so. He finds the ketchup bottle in the fridge. He squirts a load of ketchup onto his plate, then returns the bottle to the fridge. He resumes eating.

BRENDA re-enters on the phone, now holding architectural blueprints. As she speaks, she moves both breakfast plates to the sideboard so she can spread out her blueprints on the table. JASON follows his plate and resumes eating standing up at the sideboard.)

BRENDA. *(cont.)* Well Edmonton Mall is a mall. Not a state of the art shopping experience. There are no sculptures in the Edmonton Mall. There are no paintings in the Edmonton Mall... Well if they want the Edmonton mall, tell them to build the Edmonton Mall...

(to JASON) Get dressed please.

JASON. Mom, I was on level—

BRENDA. I only paused it. Hurry up.

(JASON exits.)

BRENDA. *(to phone)* "Look, I'm moving out there in less than a month and a half, and we agreed at least the foundation would be down by the time I get there. But that can't happen if you keep changing the brief you originally gave me... This won't be done by next fall, and you can forget about a 9th of the 9th 1999 ribbon-cutting date at this rate...Look, I need to think about this and call you back...Yes. I will. Bye.

(BRENDA hangs up. Then dials.)

Hi, Mrs Pitre, it's Brenda Kapowitz, Jason's mom. Again. Could you call me back please? Remember you were going to check if the disability officer could rearrange, maybe there's been a cancellation or – I really don't want to delay Jason getting a statement but this week hasn't quite gone to plan, well that's an understatement. As you know. Or maybe you don't. Who knows? But as I haven't heard from you I'm gonna assume it's still Friday or nada, as you said, well I don't think you said 'nada' but you definitely said – so ignore this message, as I will see you Friday.

(She hangs up. Some moments)

(**JASON** *enters – dressed.)*

You look nice. Bag. Game.
What?

JASON. I really don't want to go Mom.

BRENDA. Please don't start, sweetie.

JASON. Just for today. Please.

BRENDA. Jason, you can't just not go to school.

JASON. Matthew doesn't have to go.

BRENDA. Put this on.

> *(***BRENDA*** hands him his winter hat.* **JASON** *puts his bag and hat on the floor defiantly.)*

Jason, pick up your things please.

JASON. I can help too. I can clean or whatever you want.

BRENDA. That's very sweet, honey. But I don't need your help today. I've got lots to do, okay. And it's better if you're not in the way, okay.

JASON. Do I get in the way?

BRENDA. No, that's not what I meant. It's just better, alright, if I have the house to myself.

JASON. But you won't. Matthew's here.

BRENDA. Pick up your things please. Jason, you'll miss your bus and it won't be much fun walking all the way there in the cold.

JASON. I don't want to go.

BRENDA. *(takes the video game)* Shall I take this back? Jason? Shall I take this back to the store?

JASON. You can't take it back, it's been opened.

BRENDA. Jason.

JASON. People were saying things.

(*Pause. He puts on his hat.*)

BRENDA. Thank you.

JASON. Will you walk me to the bus stop?

BRENDA. What? You like walking by yourself. You're my responsible little man, right?

JASON. But there's all those, I don't want to with all those people there.

BRENDA. Well, that's why you have James.

JASON. Jimmy.

BRENDA. Jimmy will make sure that no one bothers you getting to the bus, right?

JASON. I don't like Jimmy.

BRENDA. Don't be silly.

JASON. I want you to walk with me.

BRENDA. It's just down the street.

JASON. I'll go to school. I just want you to walk with me.

BRENDA. I can't Jason.

JASON. Why not?

BRENDA. No. I can't.

JASON. It's just to the bus stop.

BRENDA. You'll be fine.

JASON. I don't want to go by myself.

BRENDA. You won't. You've got Jimmy.

JASON. He doesn't like me.

BRENDA. Nonsense.

JASON. He doesn't.

BRENDA. Did he say that?

JASON. No.

BRENDA. Well then.

JASON. I can just tell.

BRENDA. You're eight years old. Right, Jason. You can do / this.

JASON. / But I'm scared.

BRENDA. You need to do this for Mom. *(puts his coat on him)*

JASON. Mom, please just –

BRENDA. You just have to walk to the bus stop, okay? No one will touch you and –

JASON. But they –

BRENDA. I'll be watching from the window. You just have to keep walking. To the bus stop.

JASON. But Mom –

BRENDA. We'll see how fast you can go. I'll time you. Ready.

JASON. But Mom –

BRENDA. Have a good day, okay? Jason, okay? You have a good day, okay?

I've started the timer. On your marks, get set, go.

(She opens the side door, hiding behind it. **JASON** *doesn't move.*

The flash of cameras and noise of reporters suddenly filters through the open door.

JASON *starts to turn back to* **BRENDA** *but she shakes her head, points to her watch. He steps out and she quickly shuts the door behind him. She peers through the blinds.*

The phone rings once. Stops – it's been answered.

BRENDA *looks at the caller ID on the phone, quickly picks up.)*

Mum? ...Matthew, hang up the phone please... hang up the phone... Hi Mum... no, it's me Mum... yes, he answered the phone, but it's me now.... he has the day off... the teachers have meetings and things... well Bella's granddaughter doesn't go to the same school as Matthew... sorry, Mum, I haven't had a chance to... they want to see you too... Yeah, Mom, listen I have another call... call waiting, yeah Mom... Yep, I'll call you back. Bye. *(hangs up)*

(She peers through the blinds again.

She touches the second plate of breakfast food, feels it's cold, then dumps the food in the garbage.

She puts the plate in the dishwasher, and turns it on.

It starts. **BRENDA** *holds on to the machine, feeling its vibrations for a moment.*

She then sits back down and stares at the same newspaper as at the start.

The house phone rings.)

BRENDA. *(cont.) (hesitates, then answers)* Hello?

(Beat. She hangs up.)

(blackout)

Scene Two

(Kitchen. Late that afternoon.

BRENDA *stands.* **ROBERT** *sits.* The Toronto Sun *newspaper lies on the table.)*

BRENDA. I can't do that.

ROBERT. It's not a matter of what you can't do, Brenda. It's a matter of what you have to.

BRENDA. Well I won't. I mean... *(She reads from the paper.)* ... – "my active role in promoting"... I mean it's bullshit. Just / pure

ROBERT. / Which is why you have to ignore / it

BRENDA. / I didn't buy it for him.

ROBERT. This was to be expected.

BRENDA. What? That his grade nine math teacher's going to start claiming that I – I could sue them. For slander.

ROBERT. That's not a good idea.

BRENDA. We could though, right?

ROBERT. We can't get distracted, Brenda.

BRENDA. But we could. I could. If I wanted to.

ROBERT. If you can prove it completely isn't true.

BRENDA. It isn't.

ROBERT. So it didn't happen?

BRENDA. It has nothing do with anything. It's completely unrelated.

ROBERT. But did it happen?

BRENDA. Did Matthew bring a porn magazine to school when he was fifteen?

ROBERT. Did you let him?

BRENDA. You don't *let* a fifteen year-old boy do anything. He just does it.

(beat)

I told him he shouldn't have. What was I supposed to do? I didn't *(grabs paper from* **ROBERT***, reads)* "encourage" it for Christ's sake. It's...she's taking it out of context.

ROBERT. You can't let this get to you.

BRENDA. You have, haven't you?

ROBERT. ...

BRENDA. I don't mean now. But when you were a teenager. Of course you did, right? Of course you did. And when did you start? What was the first time you looked at porn?

ROBERT. It's not the issue at hand, Brenda.

BRENDA. It's the very issue at hand. Tell me. I'm asking as a friend. When?

ROBERT. Just listen to me.

BRENDA. When you answer my question. When? What, twelve, sixteen, seventeen?

Ballpark figure.

(beat)

ROBERT. I don't know. Fourteen.

BRENDA. Fourteen. Exactly. And that was even before the internet. And I'm sure there were plenty of times when your mother found whatever you were looking at. It doesn't mean...

ROBERT. Of course not. But...

BRENDA. But what?

ROBERT. Did you buy it for him?

BRENDA. Of course not!

ROBERT. Then maybe libel...not now, but afterwards, you can consider –

BRENDA. They were going to suspend him. Just for – Jesus it was two years ago.

They were going to suspend him and I...so I said it was my fault for not – they were going to suspend him for a week. It would have been on his school record. Who would have given him a university place with a suspension?

And because – fuck – two years ago and it's not – so I said...that it was my fault. Because he'd bought it on my credit card. Not to suspend him.

ROBERT. You told the school you bought it for him on / your

BRENDA. / No. He did. He did. I gave him my credit card for emergencies, for when he went out and he went online and and and I didn't say anything. When I realized, on my bill – what was I going to do? Have that conversation with my teenage son?

ROBERT. So you...?

BRENDA. So I paid the bill. The bills. A couple times. At least the delivery was free. That was a joke. He was a fifteen year old boy, right? It's normal. So I said, to the school, not to take it out on Matthew, to blame me for not, for allowing him to buy it without consequences. That's what – I didn't buy it for him, Robert.

ROBERT. Alright.

BRENDA. I didn't – they've completely taken it out of context.

ROBERT. Which is why you have to ignore it. Take a breath.

BRENDA. They're twisting it. She is twisting it. She's making it sound like –

Who writes this crap?

They're effectively saying I did this to those girls.

ROBERT. The less we see you as a mother, the less we see Matthew as a child.

(**BRENDA** *gets out the phone book. Starts looking through it. Quickly. Venomously.*)

What are you looking for?

BRENDA. I'm going to call her. I'm going to call this bitch. This Mrs. Saunders. They don't even give her first name.

ROBERT. Brenda.

BRENDA. There's a million Saunders in here.

ROBERT. Leave it.

BRENDA. Get her to take it back. Make a statement, apologize, something.

ROBERT. The damage on this one is done.

BRENDA. The damage is not "done."

(**ROBERT** *takes the phone book from her.*)

ROBERT. Brenda.

BRENDA. Give it back.

Give it back.

I am not a child!

(*He gives it back.*

BRENDA *continues flipping through the pages.*

Then stops herself.)

We have put too much into this. I won't have it ruined by some woman, some teacher, looking for her fifteen minutes.

ROBERT. Trust me on this, Brenda.

BRENDA. I do trust you. I have done everything you said. And what the hell did it matter?

ROBERT. If you get emotional, fight back, anything, you will play right into their hands.

BRENDA. So you expect me to completely ignore this?

ROBERT. I don't know if that's the right move either.

BRENDA. Move. This isn't a game, Robert. This is Matthew's life. My life.

ROBERT. This is a game. Business is a game, Brenda. Selling papers is a game. This case is a game. And whether you want to be or not, you are a key player.

BRENDA. What's our move then? Huh? What do we say?

ROBERT. We don't say anything. Acknowledging it at all admits there's even an ounce of validity.

BRENDA. So what the hell do you expect me / to

ROBERT. / Be patient.

BRENDA. I have been patient for a week! You promised me it would stop – they'd get bored. You promised if I just did my hair, my make-up, you promised if I... this is bullshit. You promised. You sat at this very table and you – you promised me, Robert!

ROBERT. Your son raped three women in one night.

(beat)

I can't control everything that happens because of it.

(Pause. **ROBERT** *pours some more coffee.)*

Would you like some?

*(***BRENDA*** *shakes her head.)*

That's not like you.

BRENDA. Let me fix this, Robert.

ROBERT. Calling his ninth grade teacher isn't going to fix this.

BRENDA. Then tell me what to do. I will fix this. Make it go away.

ROBERT. Whether we like it or not, for the next week there may be pictures. Of you. The best we can do now is embrace that. Take a more active role.

BRENDA. What exactly are you proposing I do? Pose?

ROBERT. Not exactly. What are your plans the next few days?

BRENDA. My plans?

ROBERT. What will you be doing the next five days before pre-sentencing? Any plans?

BRENDA. Oh I don't know, probably go to Disneyland for a few days.

ROBERT. Will you please take this seriously, Brenda.

BRENDA. My son could end up in some hellhole penitentiary if this screws up. Please don't tell me about taking this seriously.

(short pause)

ROBERT. I'm sorry. I shouldn't have said that. I've just seen what this can do to people. What they can do. And I don't want to see it happen to you.

BRENDA. Just worry about Matthew. I can take care of myself.

ROBERT. We go beyond your looks, what you wear. Present a whole picture. Make people see you as a victim.

BRENDA. I am. A victim.

ROBERT. But that's not how they see you. You're too strong. Too...masculine.

BRENDA. That's ridiculous. It's offensive, actually.

ROBERT. In here, you can fight, get together everything we need for this application, but out there – we need to show you simply as a good, loving mother.

BRENDA. I am a good loving mother!

ROBERT. Brenda –

BRENDA. How dare you? You think what, because, what, because you know me, because you've been at my house for dinner, because Sharon and I are friends, that somehow that gives you the right to tell me – !

ROBERT. Brenda, I am just trying to help. As a friend.

BRENDA. Well, stop trying to help and do your job! I hired you as a lawyer. That's what I need. That's what Matthew needs. A lawyer. Not a friend.

ROBERT. You asked for my advice.

BRENDA. I am not on trial here!

(long pause)

The doors were unlocked.

ROBERT. What?

BRENDA. We have to remember to include that. In my statement I think I forgot to put about the dorms being unlocked.

ROBERT. Sure.

*(**BRENDA** goes to where the phonebook is. Puts it away. Produces a pile of documents.)*

BRENDA. Report cards. Awards. Grade six one doesn't seem to be here but that shouldn't make a difference.

ROBERT. That's fine.

(beat)

BRENDA. You're the only person I've spoken to. You know? No one's even called. Besides the people I've spoken to at work...there's been no one. Hard to know who your friends are sometimes.

ROBERT. They're probably just not sure what to say.

(pause)

BRENDA. What do I need to do? Whatever it is. Just tell me what I need to do and I'll do it.

ROBERT. When will Jason be home?

BRENDA. Soon. I should start on dinner.

ROBERT. Take him to Macs's on the corner. Buy some milk. And come home.

BRENDA. That's it? That's going to counter this? *(newspaper photo)*

ROBERT. Don't let them put the milk in the bag. So when you walk home you're carrying it.

*(**BRENDA** starts laughing. Can't help herself.)*

BRENDA. You're serious?

ROBERT. You need a maternal image.

BRENDA. Me carrying a carton of milk is maternal?

ROBERT. Yes. It is.

(She laughs.)

They are desperate for images, Brenda. Don't make them have to find their own.

BRENDA. I said I'd do it.

ROBERT. What time does Jason get home? Better to do it while it's still light.

BRENDA. I'll do it. But I won't bring Jason into this.

ROBERT. If you go alone, they can easily get close ups. Just your face. But if you have Jason they'll have to do a wide to get both of you, ensuring the carton of milk gets into the picture.

BRENDA. I'll bring Matthew.

ROBERT. No. We talked about that. He stays in here. Until the decision. Brenda?

BRENDA. It's not healthy for him. For anyone. To be inside all day.

ROBERT. It's just for a little bit longer. Okay? Brenda?

BRENDA. Fine. But I'm not bringing Jason. He stays out of this.

ROBERT. You have to.

BRENDA. No.

ROBERT. Brenda—

BRENDA. I will do anything if you think it will help. I will. But I will not make Jason a part of this. Any of this. We'll have to think of something else.

(pause)

ROBERT. Have you spoken to him yet?

If you don't want to –

BRENDA. I will.

ROBERT. It's just. We're running out of time.

BRENDA. I'll talk to him.

(pause)

What's the adult sentence?

ROBERT. That's not going to happen.

BRENDA. What is it anyway?

ROBERT. We will keep this in a youth court.

BRENDA. That wasn't what I asked.

ROBERT. Seven years. Ten. Could be twenty if each count runs consecutively.

(Pause. The phone rings. They both watch the phone until it stops.

JASON enters through the side door. Sound of reporters calling into the house as he enters.)

BRENDA. Hey sweetie.

JASON. How come Robert's here?

BRENDA. You shouldn't talk about people in the third person when they're in the room.

JASON. Why are you here?

ROBERT. I'm helping your mom. And Matthew.

JASON. With what? Are you going to make all those people go away?

BRENDA. How was school?

JASON. Can you help me off with my boots?

BRENDA. Of course.

Actually.

Leave them on. We need to go to Macs's. We're out of milk.

(blackout)

Transition

(The sound of overlapping news reporters/news segments with the lines below:)

The Gamma Kappa Rapists / have

/ The University of Toronto Sorrority Rapists have come / forward

/ After weeks of students in fear / for their

/ Seventeen year-old Matthew Kapowitz and eighteen year-old Dylan Schroeder came forward / on

/ Seventeen year-old Matthew Kapowitz and Dylan Schroeder have been put under house arrest until next week/ when

/ Neighbors fear he / may be

/ He will be sentenced as / a

/ Will be sentenced as a / child

/ a child. His mother has/ been

/ Brenda Kapowitz has advocated her son / be

/ The community is outraged by /

"I'm keeping watch on that / house"

/ "Think about the children."

Scene Three
Thursday

(Matthew's bedroom. Early morning.

A small TV with built-in VHS player sits on the corner of a dresser.

BRENDA *stands in the centre of the room holding a basket with clean laundry. For a moment she doesn't move.*

She puts down the basket. She starts to strip his bed sheets, but then glances out the window.

She notices some clothing on the floor. Picks up a shirt from the floor. Smells it. Throws it in the dirty laundry hamper in the corner of the room.

Picks up a pair of boxer-briefs from the floor. Holds them out in front of her for a second. Then quickly puts them into the hamper.

Beat.

She moves to his shelf. Picks up a framed picture of a slightly younger **MATTHEW** *with friends.*

MATTHEW *enters. His hair is wet. He wears only a towel around his waist.*

He watches **BRENDA** *for a moment, before she senses him there and turns around.)*

BRENDA. Oh. *(takes him in in his towel, averts her eyes)* Sorry. I'll go.

MATTHEW. No, it's fine.

*(**BRENDA** starts removing the clean, already folded, clothes from the laundry basket and goes to put them in the closet. **MATTHEW** slides on a pair of underwear under his towel and then takes off his towel.)*

I can put them away.

BRENDA. Alright.

(**BRENDA** *puts the pile down on his bed.*

As the scene continues, **MATTHEW** *slides into a pair of summer shorts and puts on deodorant – which* **BRENDA** *again tries not to watch.*)

TV's working okay then?

MATTHEW. Yeah. Definitely.

BRENDA. And the video player?

MATTHEW. Huh?

BRENDA. Have you watched any videos?

MATTHEW. No. Not yet.

BRENDA. Should try it out. Make sure. Only a fourteen day return.

(*beat*)

(**BRENDA** *takes out clean sheets [unfolded] from the laundry basket.*)

MATTHEW. I can change them later.

BRENDA. Sure.

(*She begins to fold them –* **MATTHEW** *grabs an end of the sheet and helps her fold. It's clearly a ritual they do often.*)

So / what would...

MATTHEW. / If you...what?

BRENDA. No. What were you going to say?

MATTHEW. Just. If you have things you need to do. Like if there's anywhere you need to go, don't feel – you don't need to stay home for me.

BRENDA. I know. I know.

(*short pause*)

You're not cold? Bit strange wearing shorts in December.

MATTHEW. Warm in here.

BRENDA. Could open a window.

(pause)

What would you like for dinner?

MATTHEW. Don't mind.

BRENDA. I have to go to the grocery store. If that's alright.

MATTHEW. I can come with you.

BRENDA. That's okay. Don't need to get much.

MATTHEW. I'd like to.

(beat)

Can help make dinner.

(beat)

BRENDA. I've got to go to the office too on the way. So...
What would you like?

MATTHEW. I don't mind.

(pause)

(**MATTHEW** *puts on a hooded Roots brand sweatshirt.*

The phone rings.

BRENDA *looks around. She can't find the phone. She lifts the comforter. Not there.*

MATTHEW *finds it under the pillow. Hands it to her.)*

BRENDA. Hello?

(Beat. Hangs up.)

You should throw that out.

MATTHEW. I wear it all the time.

BRENDA. It has holes in it.

MATTHEW. It's comfortable.

BRENDA. You've had it since you were about eight.

MATTHEW. Twelve.

BRENDA. You should throw it out.

MATTHEW. I love this sweatshirt.

Just don't make them the same.

BRENDA. Think they still make the same ones, same design. Could buy a new one.

MATTHEW. No point. *(pause)* While I still have this one.

(pause)

I need to buy Jason something.

BRENDA. ...

MATTHEW. For Hanukkah.

BRENDA. Oh. I'll pick something up.

MATTHEW. I need to buy you something.

BRENDA. I'll pick something up.

(He smiles.)

MATTHEW. I'll wrap it.

BRENDA. Why did you do it?

(long pause)

JASON. *(off)* Mom!

(pause)

*(**BRENDA** picks up the laundry basket and leaves his room.*

MATTHEW turns on the TV. "I don't want to wait" by Paula Cole, the theme tune of Dawson's Creek, blasts out.

He looks at himself in the mirror.

He begins doing pushups on the floor. Joey and Dawson on the TV begin talking.

The phone rings. And continues do so as...

Lights fade to black.)

Transition

(The sound of voices from a TV.)

FEMALE VOICE 1. Well I think it goes to show she's got to carry on. There's another son to think about. A parent has to take responsibility for their children. And part of doing that is still caring for other children even if you have a crisis with one.

FEMALE VOICE 2. So are you saying she is vindicating her role as a mother, as a parent?

FEMALE VOICE 1. No. I mean I am hesitant to read too much into this. I can only imagine what's going on in her head. But I would say that she recognizes there are things she needs to do.

FEMALE VOICE 2. Thank you, Sophie Lee from the Toronto Parent and Community Network. We go back to Donald Raimer from Parents for Change. Donald, you were telling us earlier about the role of parenting especially in the teenage years as opposed to an emphasis on the primary years.

Scene Four

(Living Room. Early evening.

There is a couch, TV, coffee table. A bookshelf. Stairs leading upstairs. One door is the front door leading outside, with a mail slot. Another door leads to the kitchen. A hallway leads off to where there is a laundry room and washroom.

A large pile of mail is scattered by the front door.

JASON *is watching TV. [It is the continuation of the transition news.]*

He's eating cookies, and drinking pop.)

*(*TV:*)*

MALE VOICE 1. Potentially I came on too strong earlier. I mean this is a single parent here, there is a lot of pressure on single parents. But could this have been prevented still? I'd say yes.

(There is the brief and sudden sound of reporters voices from the kitchen. Then a door shutting firmly.

A moment later **BRENDA** *enters carrying a couple bags, taking off her winter coat.)*

*(*TV CONT'D:*)*

FEMALE VOICE 2. And where do fathers fit in to all this? I mean in this particular case, where does the father fit in?

BRENDA. We're having dinner soon. Why are you eating those?

JASON. I was hungry.

(As the TV continues **BRENDA** *notices it and is drawn in.)*

*(*TV CONT'D:*)*

MALE VOICE 1. I don't know with the particular incident of the Kapowitz's but I imagine we'll just have to keep watching.

FEMALE VOICE 2. If you've just tuned in, these images are the latest of the mother of one of the alleged rapists. Seen here with her younger son. We have yet to see Matthew himself, the alleged rapist, but on his current bail until he is sentenced next week, he is under house arrest and can only leave his house with a parent or his lawyer.

(**BRENDA** *takes the remote, attempts to change channels. Presses harder, anxiously. Nothing.*)

BRENDA. It won't...why the hell won't it...

JASON. It's not on TV. It's a video.

BRENDA. What?

(**JASON** *picks up another remote and presses a button. The TV sound stops.*)

JASON. It's a tape.

(**JASON** *retrieves it from the VHS Player.*)

BRENDA. Who gave you that?

JASON. No one. I taped it.

BRENDA. ...

JASON. When I came home I saw you on TV. So I recorded it.

BRENDA. ...

JASON. And there's one part you can see my arm! Well, the sleeve of my jacket – cause I'm holding your hand.

BRENDA. Can I have the tape please?

JASON. Why?

BRENDA. Can I have it please?

JASON. I'm bringing it to school.

BRENDA. Excuse me?

JASON. For show and tell.

BRENDA. ...

Can I have the tape please?

JASON. Why?

BRENDA. Jason, you can't...I don't think this would be the best thing for show and tell.

JASON. Why not?

BRENDA. Jason –

JASON. They'll be so jealous.

BRENDA. It's just your sleeve. I'll help you think of something else.

JASON. I don't want anything else. I'm bringing in the video.

BRENDA. You can't do that, Jason.

JASON. Sure I can.

BRENDA. It's not appropriate.

JASON. But no one can say anything mean then. Not after they see I'm on TV.

BRENDA. If someone says something, you tell your teacher, remember? Now give me the tape please.

JASON. No.

BRENDA. Jason.

JASON. It's mine. I recorded it.

BRENDA. Give it to me now!

(**JASON** *puts it behind his back.*)

Jason, I don't have time for this. I need to start dinner.

(*pause*)

I'll help you think of something else, okay.

JASON. Nothing that's this sick.

BRENDA. It's not...it's not cool. Okay? It seems like it is but it's not. And you need to stop saying "sick", it doesn't... just give me the tape, Jason.

JASON.

BRENDA. If you're going to act like a baby.

(**BRENDA** *walks over to him and reaches for it, but* **JASON** *turns his body to block it.*

He continues to successfully avoid her hands.

BRENDA *finally pins him down, trying to pry it from his hands.)*

JASON. Ow. You're hurting me. Ow. Mom.

(**JASON** *hits her on the arm.)*

BRENDA. Fine. *(retreats)*

*(***BRENDA** *grabs two wrapped presents from the bags she carried in. Holds them out to him.)*

Do you want your Hanukkah presents or not?

(pause)

Well?

(**JASON** *hands her the tape.)*

Thank you.

(She hands him the presents.)

JASON. Can I open them now?

BRENDA. If you like.

(He unwraps one of the presents. **BRENDA** *hides the video tape on a bookshelf. Then she gathers up the mail.*

JASON *has his gift unwrapped. It's a child-friendly digital camera.)*

JASON. Wow. It's wicked. *(takes the camera out of its box)*

BRENDA. And...

JASON. And...it's really wicked.

BRENDA. I meant thank you.

JASON. Thanks, Mom.

*(***BRENDA** *turns away from the door, now facing* **JASON** *again. He snaps a photo of her. She instinctively recoils.)*

Wicked! *(goes to take another)* Smile, Mom.

(She doesn't look at the camera. She retrieves three shoeboxes with letters in them, and places the new post beside them.

She opens the first letter. Reads quickly.

Puts it specifically in one of the boxes.

Starts on a second.)

Are they all for you?

BRENDA. No. Some are for Matthew.

JASON. Why are you putting them in boxes?
Mom?

(flash of camera)

BRENDA. Can you stop – why don't you take a photo of someone else?

JASON. There's no one else here.

(JASON flashes another photo.)

BRENDA. Jason you don't want to waste all the batteries already.

JASON. How do you know which letter goes in which box?
Mom?

BRENDA. Can you put those cookies away, please?

JASON. Are you coming to my school for a meeting tomorrow?

BRENDA. Yes.

JASON. Will I see you?

BRENDA. No. I don't think so.

JASON. Can I read one of the letters?

BRENDA. No.

JASON. Why? Because people are swearing at you in them?
Not like I've not heard the words before.

BRENDA. Aren't you going to open your other present?

JASON. Is it from Matthew?

BRENDA. Yes.

(He rips it open. It's a video game.)

JASON. Formula 1 98! It's the one I wanted! Sick!
Can you open it for me?
Please?...Mom?....Mom?

BRENDA. Hmm?

JASON. I can't open it.

BRENDA. Oh. *(She starts to open it, still distracted.)*

JASON. This is way sicker than Dino-Racer that Brandon and I were playing in the car today.

BRENDA. Uh-huh...what did you say?

JASON. Just I like / this

BRENDA. / When were you in Brandon's car?

JASON. Tonight.

BRENDA. Tonight...shit...shit, Thursday, shit. How did you get home? Did Brandon's mom drive you home?

*(**JASON** takes the open game, and during the following puts it in the console, and sets up the game.)*

JASON. Yeah.

BRENDA. I completely...how did she know to – why didn't you call me?

(Picks up cell, dials.)

JASON. Mr. Sams tried to after the game, but there was no answer. So he called Brandon's mom.

BRENDA. Damn it, Jason. You should've called me. Should've, shit... Shit...Hi Laura, you must be on the phone. It's Brenda, so sorry about today, I completely forgot. Thanks for getting them. Listen, I'll get the next two weeks, okay? Give me a call back. Sorry again. *(hangs up)*
Jason, who was there?

JASON. What do you mean?

BRENDA. After the game.

JASON. I don't know.

BRENDA. I mean does anybody else know I wasn't, that I forgot to come.

JASON. I don't know.

BRENDA. Jason, can you just pause it for a second. Jason, I need you to think okay? What about Michael's mom?

Or Jonathan's? Were they there?

JASON. I don't know, Mom.

BRENDA. Where did she, where did Brandon's mom drop you off?

JASON. Here.

BRENDA. No, I mean, did she drive into the driveway? Was it down the street?

JASON. On the street, cause there were too many cars and stuff to get by.

BRENDA. Did they see?

JASON. Did who see?

BRENDA. Were any of the...did anyone see that Brandon's mom dropped you off? Anyone talk to her?

JASON. Don't think so. Maybe one guy.

BRENDA. Shit. Who? Jason, who?

JASON. I don't know.

BRENDA. Well think. What did he look like?

JASON. I don't remember.

(**BRENDA** *grabs the controls from his hand.*)

Hey!

BRENDA. What did he look like, Jason? Was it the CBC guy?

JASON. I'm going to lose the race.

BRENDA. I need to know who it was, Jason!

(**JASON**'s *hindering on a crying outburst.*)

BRENDA. Jason.

JASON. I don't know!

(*She hands him back the controls.*)

BRENDA. Okay. That's fine. Sorry Jason. I just...I just needed to know. (*kisses his head*) Sorry I yelled.

(*pause*)

(*She starts to dial on the phone. Stops herself.*)

Jason. Honey, can you do something for me?

JASON. What?

BRENDA. Could you call Brandon?

JASON. Why?

BRENDA. Just call him, to say hello. And if he's not there, just leave him a message to call you back. Come on Jason, it'll be nice.

JASON. But I don't have anything to say to him.

BRENDA. You could talk about school.

JASON. What about school?

BRENDA. I don't know...something, anything. What you did at recess.

JASON. But I was with him at recess, so why would we need to talk about it.

BRENDA. And when you're done talking to Brandon, then you can just pass the phone to me and I can talk to Laura.

JASON. Why don't you just call Laura then?

BRENDA. I did sweetie, but sometimes it takes adults a while to call back, right? Can you do this for me?

JASON. I'm in the middle of a race.

BRENDA. Just pause it for a second. Jason.

> *(beat)*

> You can talk at the same time, can't you? That would help Mom a lot.

> *(She dials. Puts the phone in the crook of his neck while he plays.)*

> There you go.

JASON. There's no one there.

BRENDA. Leave a message.

JASON. Hi Brandon. Guess you're not there. See you at school tomorrow. Bye. *(hangs up)*

BRENDA. You were supposed to tell him to call you back! You didn't even say who it was.

JASON. I can tell him tomorrow.

BRENDA. Thanks a lot, Jason.

> *(The phone rings.)*
>
> *(**BRENDA** grabs it.)*
>
> Hello?...
>
> *(Pause. She hangs up.)*

JASON. Was that Brandon?

BRENDA. No.

> *(beat)*

JASON. They kept saying our last name wrong. They kept saying Ka-POW-itz. *(does an imitation of reporter)* Brenda Ka-POW-itz, Brenda Ka-POW-itz. *(He giggles at the voice he's doing.)* Is it still snowing?

> *(**BRENDA** exits to the kitchen.*
>
> *JASON takes another cookie.*
>
> *He moves to the window, peeks out.)*
>
> Mom! Mom! *(pause)* Mom!
>
> *(He takes the Hanukkia [menorah] from the bookshelf and puts it on the side table.)*
>
> Mom!
>
> *(**BRENDA** enters.)*

BRENDA. What? What is it Jason?

JASON. It's almost dark. We need to light the candles.

BRENDA. Oh. Fine. Right.

JASON. Matthew!

BRENDA. It's fine. Leave him. We can do it the two of us. *(starts looking for menorah)* I...I can't find –

JASON. I already set it up.

BRENDA. Oh. *(strokes his hair)* That's lovely.

> *(She starts picking at the dried wax in the candle holders of the menorah.)*
>
> You know every year I say I should clean out the wax so it's ready for next year, and every year I don't. I'll get

the candles.

(BRENDA *exits to the kitchen as* MATTHEW *comes downstairs.* JASON *begins looking through a drawer.*)

JASON. Do you know where my kipa is? It's only yours in here.

MATTHEW. You can wear mine.

JASON. What will you wear?

MATTHEW. I'll wear something else.

(JASON *puts on the kipa.*)

JASON. Thanks for the game, Matthew. I love it.

MATTHEW. ...Good. I'm glad.

JASON. Do you wanna race me later?

MATTHEW. Maybe.

(MATTHEW *gets a party hat from the drawer. Puts it on his head.*)

JASON. What are you doing?

MATTHEW. Have to cover my head with something.

JASON. It's from like my 6th birthday.

MATTHEW. So?

JASON. You look like an idiot.

MATTHEW. Well then, give me back my kipa and you can wear this.

(BRENDA *reenters. She sees* MATTHEW, *doesn't acknowledge him.*)

BRENDA. I...we don't have any Hanukkah candles.
I'll get some tomorrow.

(MATTHEW *exits to the kitchen.*)

JASON. But what about tonight? You can't just skip the first night.

BRENDA. I'm sorry, Jason. But we don't have any candles. Okay?

JASON. Everyone else will be talking at school tomorrow

about lighting their candles. Everyone.

BRENDA. Well, we're not everyone, Jason.

JASON. But I'll be left out.

BRENDA. You can pretend. Just picture it from last year.

JASON. I should lie?

(MATTHEW *reenters with some birthday candles.*)

Mom wants me to lie.

MATTHEW. Here.

JASON. You can't use those.

BRENDA. Matthew's right. They're virtually the same. Come on. You put them in Jason. Hurry up. It'll be completely dark in a second.

(JASON *puts two of the candles in.*

MATTHEW *lights the "Shamash" using a lighter.*)

You should really use matches.

(MATTHEW *lifts the Shamash and goes to light the other candle with it.*)

JASON. Wait. We all have to do it.

MATTHEW. Well, take hold then.

(JASON *puts his hand over* MATTHEW*'s.*)

JASON. Come on, Mom.

BRENDA. I'm watching.

JASON. No, we all have to do it.

(BRENDA *stands.*)

You need to cover your head.

BRENDA. It doesn't matter.

JASON. It does. Or you'll go to hell.

BRENDA. Jews don't believe in hell.

JASON. Maybe I'm not Jewish then.

BRENDA. Then why are you lighting Hanukkah candles?

(*She retrieves another party hat. Puts it on her head.*)

Here. Okay.

JASON. You have to hold on like we always do.

(**BRENDA** *slightly hesitates then takes hold of the candle over* **MATTHEW**'s *hand. As they sing they light the candle.*)

BRENDA. You have to sing, Jason.

JASON. *(sings)* Barukh Atta Adonay...

I can't remember the rest.

MATTHEW. *(sings)* Eloheynu Melekh Ha-olam

Asher Kiddeshanu Be-mitsvotav

Ve-tsivanu

Lehadlik Ner

ALL 3. *(sing)* Shel khanuka

BRENDA. Amen.

JASON. Oh, wait.

(**JASON** *grabs his new camera.*)

BRENDA. Oh not right now, Jason. Jason.

JASON. Just one. You have to move closer.

(**BRENDA** *and* **MATTHEW** *move in but don't touch. The menorah is in front of them, the party hats are still on both their heads.*)

You have to smile...come on...

(*They force a smile.*)

Say...um...say Happy Hanukkah!

BOTH. *(with little emotion, still forced-smiling)* Happy Hanukkah.

(*flash*)

(*blackout*)

Scene Five

(The living room. Late at night.

MATTHEW *watches TV. He is watching infomercials on the shopping channel.*

JASON *comes downstairs in pajamas.)*

JASON. What are you watching?

MATTHEW. I'm not...really... Why aren't you in bed?

JASON. I can't sleep.

(pause)

MATTHEW. You should probably try to sleep. *(pause)* You'll be tired at school.

JASON. We have a supply teacher tomorrow.

MATTHEW. Mom know you're still up?

JASON. No.

MATTHEW. You should go to your room. She won't be happy if she finds you down here.

JASON. She's sleeping. I already checked.

(pause)

Can you not sleep either?

MATTHEW. Haven't tried yet.

(Pause. Just the sound of the TV.)

JASON. You gonna buy that?

MATTHEW. No.

JASON. Cause I think Mom bought one already.

(pause)

MATTHEW. Do you want me to read to you?

JASON. Read what?

MATTHEW. I dunno. A book. Help you fall asleep.

JASON. I'm not a baby.

MATTHEW. Well. You should try to sleep. Think I'll go to bed soon.

JASON. Think it's the light. Too many lights. When do you think they'll leave?

MATTHEW.

JASON. I can hear them talking sometimes too. Not the words. But sometimes when they're smoking at the side, by my window, I hear them. *(beat)* If I tell you something, promise you won't tell Mom?
Promise?

MATTHEW. What?

JASON. You have to promise.

MATTHEW. Okay. What?

JASON. I heard these two. I opened my window and they were saying stuff. About us. And this one, he was holding his camera or something. A video camera, you know? And he put it down and went away for a few seconds...so I got my water cup, the water beside my bed and poured it out the window. Onto his camera.

MATTHEW. Seriously?

(*JASON nods.*)

You shouldn't've done that.

(**MATTHEW** *starts laughing. Then* **JASON** *does too. A moment.*)

You shouldn't've done that, Jason. Seriously. Don't do it again. Promise, or I'll tell Mom.

JASON. You promised.

MATTHEW. Then you promise.

JASON. Okay. I won't.

(beat)

Do you want to play "Formula One"?

(**JASON***'s already setting up the game on the TV.*)

MATTHEW. I think I need to sleep.

JASON. Please.

MATTHEW. Can't you play against the machine?

JASON. It's not as fun. And it's impossible to win against the machine.

MATTHEW. You might not win against me either.

JASON. Yeah I will. *(hands MATTHEW the controls)*

MATTHEW. Turn it down. Where are you going?

JASON. Just a sec. You have to choose a car. *(exits to kitchen)*

(MATTHEW concentrates, chooses a car.)

(JASON reenters with a can of supermarket-brand pop.)

MATTHEW. Mom's gonna kill you.

JASON. What?

I'm allowed.

Do you want some?

MATTHEW. That stuff tastes like shit.

JASON. No it doesn't. Do you want me to explain how to play?

MATTHEW. I know how to play.

JASON. Here we go.

MATTHEW. Turn the volume down. Jason. You'll wake up Mom.

JASON. After this round.

(They both concentrate as they play, and instantly get into the game.)

Hey, you're in my lane!

MATTHEW. You're in mine!

JASON. Hey!

MATTHEW. Hey yourself! *(starts laughing)*

(pause)

JASON. Yes. Yes. I'm so beating you.

(MATTHEW jabs him playfully with one hand, while he continues to play the game with the other. They're both laughing.)

Hey. Hey stop.

(**MATTHEW** *drops his controls and tickles* **JASON**.)

(**BRENDA** *enters on the stairs. Stands there, unnoticed, watching them.*)

JASON. *(cont.)* Hey, that's cheating.

MATTHEW. Says who?

JASON. Matthew!

(**MATTHEW** *picks up controls again; he's back in the game.* **JASON** *grabs* **MATTHEW**'s *controls, sits on them, and continues to play with his own.*)

MATTHEW. That's not fair Jason. Jason.

(He tries to get them back, unsuccessfully.

JASON keeps playing for a moment and then gives back the controls.)

JASON. Here you go.

(A few seconds later, **JASON** *wins the game.)*

Yes. Yes. Yes.

MATTHEW. You cheated.

JASON. You cheated first.

MATTHEW. Yeah, but I lost.

JASON. Guess you're not a very good cheater then. Two out of three?

MATTHEW. No. Thanks.

(**BRENDA** *goes back upstairs, again unnoticed.*)

JASON. Please.

MATTHEW. Maybe tomorrow. Try to sleep now. Go on.

JASON. Do you think I'll be in the paper?

(pause)

(**JASON** *goes to put the pop away.)*

MATTHEW. I'll do it.

JASON. Goodnight Matthew.

(**JASON** *goes upstairs.*

Pause.

MATTHEW *has a sip of the pop.)*
(He begins to play the Formula 1 game again.)
(fade out)

Transition

(Two different radio programmes.)

DJ 1. T-G-I-F! Good morning Toronto. It's 7 / a.m.

DJ 2. It's 7 am Friday morning. Today's headlines.

DJ 1. I've got your daily dose of news. Looking at today's / headlines.

DJ 2. In the Toronto Star "Smiling Rapist" is our headline / with a photo.

DJ 1. Toronto Sun. "Mom Throws Rapist a Party and Abandons Younger Son" with a / photo

DJ 2. With a photo of Gamma Kappa Rapist Matthew Kapowitz with his mother / smiling.

DJ 1. Smiling with party hats on their heads and what looks like the top of birthday candles.

DJ 2. First images of him to emerge since his house / arrest.

DJ 1. Family of one of the victims outraged that he's having a party while their daughter is suffering.

DJ 2. In other news last night was the first night of the Jewish Festival of Lights, celebrating the miracle when –

DJ 1. Day 2 of Operation Desert Fox. Is this just a distraction tactic for Clinton's Impeachment proceedings asks the Sun.

(And the radio sound is overpowered by the sound of internet dial-up...)

Scene Six
Friday

(The Living Room. Midday.

Architectural blueprints are spread across the coffee table, along with a mug of coffee.

BRENDA *enters from the kitchen, with a large bag. She dumps the contents of the bag onto the coffee table: newspapers – every daily.*

She reads part of the cover of one paper, then throws it down to the floor. She does the same with the next. The next. Each time quicker and angrier than the last.

She suddenly starts to dry wretch into her hand. She runs off to the kitchen. We can hear her vomiting.

She reenters with a glass of water.

Sits. A moment.

She sips her coffee – spits it back into the mug – it's cold.

She sits back, and puts herself in rescue position. A moment.

Retrieves a scrapbook and scissors.

Begins cutting out the photo from the paper and gluing it into her scrapbook.

Her mobile rings. She looks at the number, lets it ring, and continues her craft.

Once finished, she begins rushing to get ready. She puts on her coat, glances in a hall mirror.)

BRENDA. Shit.

(She tosses off her shoes. Opens the hall closet and ruffles through. She finds one shoe and puts it on. Rummages some more and finds the matching second shoe. Puts it on. Grabs her purse, one last

glance in the mirror, and she opens the front door.

JESSICA *is standing on the other side, about to ring the bell. She carries a small book bag.)*

(BRENDA *lets out a small yelp. Flash, flash.)*

BRENDA. *(cont.)* Jessica. God. You scared me.

JESSICA. Sorry.

(pause)

BRENDA. It's good to see you.

(pause)

JESSICA. Can I come in?

BRENDA. Yes, of course. Come in, come in, I was just... *(both inside, she closes the door)* I'm actually on my way out to Jason's school though.

JESSICA. Now's not a good time, then?

BRENDA. *(jokily)* I think the notion of "good time" has lost all meaning.

(JESSICA does not respond.)

How are you?

(pause)

JESSICA. I left a message. Well two. He hasn't called back.

BRENDA. Did you?

JESSICA. Yes.

BRENDA. Probably just hasn't listened to them yet. The phone's been ringing a lot. As you can probably imagine.

(silence)

JESSICA. *(looking at blueprints)* Oh. Is this the mall you're doing?

BRENDA. Yes.

JESSICA. Have they started building yet?

BRENDA. No. Not yet.

JESSICA. Wow, it looks...wow. Though you shouldn't bring your work home with you, that's what they say isn't it? Or not do work in your living room or bedroom or else you can never relax there. So I generally work in my dad's study.

(pause)

I brought you something. *(holds out an envelope)*

(Pause. BRENDA *hesitantly takes it.)*

Aren't you going to open it?

*(*BRENDA *does. It's a card.)*

Happy Hanukkah. Starts today doesn't it?

BRENDA. Last night. Yes. Thank you. That was very thoughtful.

JESSICA. Did you make those potato pancakes again this year?

BRENDA. No.

JESSICA. Oh. Well. I guess you still can. Eight nights, isn't there?

BRENDA. What?

JESSICA. Hanukkah. Nice to have eight nights.

BRENDA. I just...I'm actually a bit late. I need to be going.

JESSICA. Oh. Right. Well. Don't stay on my account, Ms. Kapowitz.

(pause)

He upstairs?

(silence)

We never had sex you know.
We didn't.

BRENDA. You don't have to tell me that.

JESSICA. We didn't though. And now I...maybe that's why, right? I mean it makes sense. Matthew said he was okay with it, that there was no rush, that, and now... *(starts to cry)* God.

(**BRENDA** *doesn't move. Just watches her until she stops.*)

(*long pause*)

JESSICA. He told me we would've had to end it this summer before we go away anyway. Avoid the turkey break-up. I just wanted to wait. We did other things though. I was fine doing other things.

BRENDA. Jessica, you don't need to –

JESSICA. It's just the sex part. That's what's been my whole belief, you know? I hoped one day it would be Matthew, but I knew it wouldn't. I mean he told me, right. You wouldn't let him marry someone who wasn't Jewish.

BRENDA. Jessica, I like you, you know that.

JESSICA. I never said you didn't, Ms. Kapowitz. You've been so nice to me, I'm not saying, I mean you have, I'm always here and, well not recently, but I'm always here and you're so kind, and you do like me. Just not to be his wife. And that's fine. It's just...oh...I don't even know what I'm saying. I'm sorry. I'm just...

Have you seen the girls?

BRENDA. Pardon?

JESSICA. Abi, Rachel, Jessica. I saw her picture. Jessica. She's pretty.

(*silence*)

JESSICA. Do you think...do you think he knew her name was also Jessica? That's what I keep thinking. She doesn't look like me or anything, but I wonder if he knows. Well he does now I guess, but if he did then.

BRENDA. Jessica, I really think you should go home.

JESSICA. Well, without being rude, Ms. Kapowitz, I'm not going anywhere.

BRENDA. Pardon me?

JESSICA. Not until I speak to him. Not until he answers the questions I have. Not until...I'm owed that much. It's my right.

(silence)

(**BRENDA**'s *mobile phone rings. She examines the number.*)

BRENDA. Shit. *(silences her phone)*

(*JESSICA makes as if to make her way to the stairs.*)

(**BRENDA** *steps into her path.*)

This really isn't a good time.

(pause)

BRENDA. I'll have him call you.

JESSICA. Did he say anything?

That night? Cause I talked to him before. Before he went out and he didn't. He seemed...normal. So I just need to know.

JESSICA. Did he say anything before he left? About me? Or about? Well about anything. What did he say?

What did he say to you? Before he went out? During dinner. Or after dinner. Or even before. What did he say to you?

He must have said something. Something. You don't just go out and

And not say anything before!

I'm sorry. I didn't mean to shout.

It's like everything...every memory, you know – like they're all different now. Like they've all been tainted or – not tainted – just changed. Retrospect. That's what it does, right? Like I can't stop analyzing all of them...like they're all some puzzle piece leading up to this act, this horrible – and I keep wondering what I missed – keep searching for the clues and it's like every memory, well they're not memories anymore, like they've been taken from me.

So I need to know, Ms Kapowitz. I have a right to know!

(Footsteps on the stairs. **MATTHEW** *appears.* **MATTHEW** *and* **JESSICA** *see each other.)*

(silence)

JESSICA. Hi.

MATTHEW. Hi.

(long pause)

How...how you've been?

(pause)

Do you want to come up?

(pause)

(**JESSICA** *nods. Starts to go to stairs.)*

BRENDA. No!

(They both look at **BRENDA.** *Even she is visibly unsure of what she's just done.)*

(**JESSICA** *continues to go again.)*

Wait! You... *(She goes to the middle of the stairs – stands between them.)*

...if you come back later, I can, you can join us for dinner. Be better to have a proper talk.

JESSICA. I'm not hungry.

BRENDA. Well no, course not, but later. For dinner, right. You'll be hungry then. Just come back then. You'll be hungry then.

JESSICA. Thank you. For the offer. But it's best if I talk to Matthew alone. *(starts to go)*

BRENDA. You can't go up there.

MATTHEW. Mom, what are you –

BRENDA. You need to go home, Jessica.

JESSICA. Ms. Kapowitz –

BRENDA. I said you need to go home.

JESSICA. I've told you, this is something I need to do.

BRENDA. And I've told you to go home. Or. Shouldn't you be in school? You're skipping school, aren't you?

MATTHEW. Mom.

BRENDA. What would your teachers say?

MATTHEW. Mom.

BRENDA. Now go home.

(pause)

JESSICA. Please, can I pass?

BRENDA. I can't let you do that.

JESSICA. This is ridiculous.

(Goes to move past, **BRENDA** *moves over, blocking her way.)*

Why are you doing this?

BRENDA. Just go home.

JESSICA. Why are you doing this?

BRENDA. Do I need to call your parents?

MATTHEW. Mom, just let her –

BRENDA. Just go.

JESSICA. I'm not going anywhere.

BRENDA. I will, I will call the police then.

JESSICA. You're going to call the police?

MATTHEW. Mom, stop it.

BRENDA. This is my house, and I've asked you to go.

MATTHEW. Mom just let her –

BRENDA. Don't you touch me.

JESSICA. I just want to –

BRENDA. Don't touch me.

MATTHEW. What are you doing? *(touches her again)* Why are you doing this?

BRENDA. Don't you touch me! Now go! Now, you stupid girl!

*(***BRENDA*** *quickly ushers* **JESSICA** *down the stairs and runs her out the front door.* **BRENDA** *shuts it*

hard behind her.)

(**BRENDA** *remains standing with her back hard against the door. A moment.)*

(A noise. The mail slot opens, and mail is dropped through. And more, and more. Letters are pouring through the slot behind **BRENDA**.*)*

(fade out)

Transition

(Sound of TV News Panel Show.)

FEMALE VOICE 1. It's an act of violence against women. It's further insult to those girls to say it was an act of a child. It diminishes the horrific nature of the experience those girls went through. In saying it was the act of a child, she's effectively taking the experience of those women away from them.

FEMALE VOICE 2. That was Doctor Lidia Marx, Professor of Women's Studies at the University of Toronto where of course all three of the victims went to school. We go live to Brian Jones to tell us about the petition that's been launched.

MALE VOICE 1. Yes, Gail, I'm standing outside the home of one of the alleged self-confessed rapists and I'm holding right now a petition signed by parents, students and really any member of the community, that's been launched in response to the mother of one of the rapists, Brenda Ka-POW-itz, who is advocating for her 17 year-old son to be sentenced as a child.

FEMALE VOICE 2. So what does this mean? Does this have any bearing on the sentencing?

MALE VOICE 1. No one's sure. In the past, some judges have weighed in a community's opinion the same way they weigh in references, personal statements, as they would for any appeal like this for someone aged 16 to 18. But effectively the Toronto community is making it clear that she's not the only one fighting here and they demand she act like a mother and ensure her son is brought to the full justice he deserves.

Scene Seven

(The living room. Early evening. Outside it is dark.

The post has not been cleared from the floor by the front door.

MATTHEW *and* **ROBERT** *sit.*

Silence.)

ROBERT. Matthew.

(silence)

This isn't going to help you. He is not helping you, Matthew. You need to think about yourself now.

MATTHEW. He's my friend.

ROBERT. And I promise you that Jack Markoffs is having the exact same conversation with his client right now. If there's anything that –

MATTHEW. I've known Dylan since I was eight.

ROBERT. You're going away. How long is up to you. You need to tell me – if there is anything, anything he said, or did that puts more of the weight on him. On Dylan. As the leader of all this. Anything at all.

(silence)

The bar you were at beforehand. O'Grady's. You hadn't been there before?

MATTHEW. Does it matter?

ROBERT. Yes.

MATTHEW. Why?

ROBERT. How about I worry about the questions, you worry about the answers. O'Grady's. You hadn't been there before, correct?

MATTHEW. Correct, Mr. Rosenberg.

ROBERT. Had Dylan?

MATTHEW. You have a crush on him or something?

(beat)

Yeah, he'd been there before.

ROBERT. How'd you get drinks?

MATTHEW. What do you mean?

ROBERT. Did one of you have a fake I.D.?

MATTHEW. No. They don't check.

ROBERT. And if they had?

MATTHEW. We knew they didn't.

ROBERT. You knew.

MATTHEW. That's what I said.

ROBERT. Because Dylan had been there before?

So you went to that bar at Dylan's suggestion because he knew they wouldn't I.D. you both, having been there before. Is that fair to say?

MATTHEW. I guess.

ROBERT. And what were you drinking?

MATTHEW. What do you think?

(beat)

Beer, alright. That detailed enough for you?

ROBERT. No actually. What kind of beer?

MATTHEW. What?

ROBERT. What brand beer were you drinking?

MATTHEW. It wasn't my fault, it was Stella Artois that did it.

ROBERT. You find this amusing, Matthew?

I am trying to help you. And if you would like to spend your twenties somewhere other than a concrete four by four, I suggest you help me too.

MATTHEW. LaBatt's.

ROBERT. Dylan was drinking that too?

*(**MATTHEW** nods.)*

Tell me about the girls. You mentioned they were at the bar.

Matthew?

MATTHEW. Yeah.

ROBERT. Were they drinking?

MATTHEW. I don't know.

ROBERT. You don't remember or –

MATTHEW. I guess so. I assume so.

ROBERT. Did you talk to them? You or Dylan?

MATTHEW. Need some air.

ROBERT. You needed some –

MATTHEW. I'd like some air. I need some air.

ROBERT. Right now I want –

MATTHEW. What about what I want? I'd like to go outside. But I'm locked in this house because you and my mother won't let me out for even five fucking minutes.

ROBERT. After we finish writing this. I promise.

MATTHEW. Whatever.

ROBERT. I promise. I do.

So you're drinking at O'Grady's and you see the girls. And then presumably they leave, and someone what, suggests you follow them?

MATTHEW. That's not what happened.

ROBERT. No one put the idea on the table.

MATTHEW. They invited us.

ROBERT. They invited you...to their rooms?

MATTHEW. Yes. No. They invited us. We didn't follow anyone.

ROBERT. I'm a bit confused Matthew because according to one of their statements they were asleep.

MATTHEW. No. They were.

ROBERT. But they invited you –

MATTHEW. No, they didn't invite us.

ROBERT. But you just said

MATTHEW. Jesus Christ, just listen to me.

ROBERT. I am listening.

MATTHEW. No one listens to me. Everyone just goes on

and on about everything to do with me but no one wants to listen to me.

ROBERT. I am listening Matthew.

They were sleeping, right? But you're saying they invited you.

MATTHEW. They didn't invite us. It wasn't the same girls.

ROBERT. There were other girls.

MATTHEW. And they invited us.

ROBERT. To the sorority? To Gamma Kappa?

Matthew?

The girls from the bar, different girls, at the bar, they invited you to their sorority, the same sorority as Abi, Rachel, Jessica.

Matthew, is that right?

These other girls, at the bar, they invited you to –

MATTHEW. I don't remember! Okay! I don't remember.

(pause)

ROBERT. Why don't we take a break. Would you like a drink?

MATTHEW.

*(**ROBERT** exits to kitchen.)*

*(**BRENDA** enters down the stairs. She wears a bathrobe and wet hair.)*

*(**MATTHEW** stands, starts to go upstairs. **BRENDA** is in his path on the stairs.)*

BRENDA. Where are you going?

MATTHEW. My room.

BRENDA. Don't you have to talk with Robert still?

MATTHEW. There isn't anything left to talk about.

BRENDA. Is that what Robert said?

MATTHEW. Yeah.

BRENDA. He did? He said you don't need to talk anymore?

MATTHEW. Didn't I just say that?

BRENDA. Don't talk to me in that tone.

MATTHEW. Don't talk to me like I'm a kid.

(beat)

(He starts to go up.)

Matthew, if Mr. Rosenberg wants to talk, you talk to him. Right now.

MATTHEW. There's nothing left to say. I've told him everything.

BRENDA. Well then, I'm sure it won't take much longer.

(They stare for a moment. He comes back down the stairs.)

*(**ROBERT** reenters with a glass of water.)*

*(**MATTHEW** exits to the washroom.)*

Matthew!

MATTHEW. I'm going to piss. Is that okay with you, Warden?

(Pause. He's out of the room.)

BRENDA. Will you be staying for dinner?

ROBERT. Uh no no. I'll be finished soon.

BRENDA. It's no problem. There'll be plenty extra. I've got a whole chicken.

ROBERT. Thanks, but Sharon's expecting me

BRENDA. Of course. I can just offer the leftovers to the masses in front of my house. Might shoot me from a favourable angle in return.

(beat)

ROBERT. He doesn't seem himself.

BRENDA. Would you?

ROBERT. But more so today.

BRENDA. Maybe the pressure's finally got to him.

ROBERT. And you?

BRENDA. I'm fine.

ROBERT. You need to sleep Brenda. You're not superwoman.

BRENDA. Who said I haven't been sleeping?

ROBERT. Your eyes.

(Beat. She goes to the mirror.)

And Jason? He's coping at school?

BRENDA. I missed his meeting. Now he hasn't been statemented and can't be for another three months which means it'll be at least – he can't get any support and they won't...when it rains it certainly fucking pours.

ROBERT. It will sort itself out.

BRENDA. Will it?

ROBERT. Tom Cruise is dyslexic.

BRENDA. And look how he turned out.

ROBERT. Okay. Bad example. *(laughs)*

BRENDA. It's not funny.

ROBERT. I wasn't laughing at – I was – about Tom Cruise.

BRENDA. I resented them. At the initial hearing. For a moment I resented them. And I hate myself for it, but I did. I do. And I keep thinking these poor girls, everything they've, what he, when it's him I should resent. But it was them I resented. I hate what he did. What he's done. But him, I can't hate. Can I? That's the curse of children, Robert.

(pause)

So after this, what happens? You and Jack Markoffs submit their applications jointly and then we just –

ROBERT. No.

Brenda...Dylan won't be sentenced as a child.

BRENDA. You can't know that. Not yet.

ROBERT. He's withdrawn his application.

BRENDA. What does this mean? Robert.

What does this mean?

ROBERT. I don't know.

BRENDA. You do know.

Dylan's going to fuck this up, isn't he? Because he –

I know his parents for God's sake. I've had them over for dinner.

ROBERT. I think this can work in our favor. Dylan understood the consequences of his actions, dragged Matthew into this. That's the angle.

BRENDA. That's the truth.

What has Dylan said? What are you not telling me?

(MATTHEW *reenters. Sits.*)

(*long pause*)

MATTHEW. Well?

ROBERT. Sorry. Brenda. Would you mind...?

BRENDA. I would actually.

ROBERT. Just makes more sense. If it were just Matthew and I. As we've already started.

BRENDA. I'd rather stay.

ROBERT. Brenda, it would be easier / if

BRENDA. / I am his mother, and he is still legally a child and I have a right to be here, don't I? So you can just carry on as if I'm not here.

(*pause*)

ROBERT. You were saying about the girls, Matthew. Who invited you to their rooms.

MATTHEW.

ROBERT. What happened at Gamma Kappa, before you broke into – before you entered Abi's room?

(*pause*)

Before you entered the room, Abi's room, did one of you suggest something?

BRENDA. Matthew, Mister Rosenberg has asked you a question.

Matthew.

MATTHEW. I don't know what you want me to say.

ROBERT. I don't *want* you to say anything. I'm just trying to understand the events as they took place.

What happened right before you entered Abi's room?

MATTHEW. When do I get to go outside?

ROBERT. Why don't we skip to after? What can you tell me about after the incidents?

Did you and Dylan talk about anything?

MATTHEW. Like what?

ROBERT. I don't know. What did you say to each other? Did he say anything about what he had just done?

MATTHEW. What *we* had done. Why are you so obsessed with Dylan?

ROBERT. I'm trying to understand.

MATTHEW. He's got his own lawyer, right? Let him worry about him.

ROBERT. Did he say how he felt afterward? Did you talk about what you'd both done?

MATTHEW. You can't blame him for everything.

ROBERT. I'm not. I'm just asking –

BRENDA. Why are you protecting him?

MATTHEW. I'm not protecting anyone.

BRENDA. Then just answer his / question.

ROBERT. / Brenda.

MATTHEW. I answered it. He didn't say anything!

BRENDA. Tell the truth, Matthew.

ROBERT. Brenda! Let me do this please.

MATTHEW. I am telling the truth!

BRENDA. So you assault three girls and all the while neither of you say a word to each other! Not during, not before, not after!

MATTHEW. Just shutup, Mom.

BRENDA. Don't you dare tell me to shutup.

ROBERT. Brenda! Let me handle this please.

BRENDA. No, let me handle this. He is my son.

They might sentence you as an adult! Do you get that? And we are trying to help you. You! So stop worrying about Dylan, or your feelings for Jessica or whatever

this is about and you answer, you answer everything
that Robert asks you or so help me God!

ROBERT. Brenda! Please.

BRENDA. Tell him it was Dylan's idea! That Dylan made
you go to the university bars that night. Tell him!

MATTHEW. It was his idea we go to those bars but it was
my idea to break into the girls' rooms!

(sudden quiet)

(long pause)

*(**BRENDA** rises and quickly lights the Hanukkah
candles – 3 in total [the shamash plus 2]. She does
not say any prayer.)*

*(**JASON** enters the front door. He wears a baseball
cap pulled down low, shadowing his upper face.)*

*(They all momentarily freeze seeing **JASON**. He
takes off his boots, head down.)*

BRENDA. Hey you. How was school?

*(**JASON** doesn't respond. Just makes his way to the
stairs. **BRENDA** goes to him.)*

Jason...?

*(She takes off his baseball cap. Underneath is a
swollen eye.)*

Oh my God. Jason, what happened?

JASON. ...

BRENDA. Jason!

JASON. Nothing... *(almost starts to cry)* Just some, some...

BRENDA. Some what?

JASON. Some kids at school. These two kids.

BRENDA. Who? Who did this? Why didn't anyone call me?
Why didn't – who did this Jason?

JASON. Michael Buchman and this kid Geoffrey. I don't
know his last name. He's in grade six.

BRENDA. Why? Why did they – what happened?

JASON. I was just, I was leaving school, and I was in the bit behind the portable and they were just there. They just pushed me down. And punched me.

They just said, "This is for Abi."

BRENDA. What?

JASON. I don't know. That's all they said before, before I kicked him in the...to get him off me, so I could run away.

BRENDA. Don't touch it. It'll...I'm calling the school. Right now.

JASON. Don't Mom. Mom, please.

BRENDA. Jason, they need to punish these kids.

JASON. Please Mom, don't.

MATTHEW. Let me see.

BRENDA. Don't. Don't touch him.

MATTHEW. I'm just –

BRENDA. Just get away from him. Matthew.

(**MATTHEW** *backs away.* **JASON** *stands there confused, scared.* **MATTHEW** *exits to the kitchen.* **BRENDA** *holds the phone, while she looks up the phone number.*)

ROBERT. Did anyone see? Anyone outside, the reporters, did they see your eye?

JASON. I was wearing my hat.

(**ROBERT** *hangs up the phone in* **BRENDA***'s hand.*)

BRENDA. What are you doing?

ROBERT. We have to think about this.

If people find out. It could affect things.

BRENDA. This has nothing to with it. Some kids beat up my son.

JASON. Mom, please don't.

ROBERT. Just wait a second. We need to think.

BRENDA. Go upstairs, Jason.

ROBERT. Brenda just hear me out.

JASON. Mom!

BRENDA. Go upstairs Jason!

ROBERT. Hear me out Brenda.

JASON. Mom!

(**MATTHEW** *runs in with ice.*)

BRENDA. I said to go upstairs Jason!

(*to* **MATTHEW***)* What are you – get away from him.

MATTHEW. He needs ice.

BRENDA. *(to* **MATTHEW***)* Just, just sit down.

MATTHEW. *(to* **JASON***)* Hold this here. *(puts his hand over his and lifts the ice to his eye)*

BRENDA. Don't touch him.

MATTHEW. I'm helping him.

BRENDA. I think you've been enough help, Matthew!

JASON. It's not Matthew's fault.

BRENDA. Jason, go upstairs! Now! Run yourself a bath. *(to* **MATTHEW***)* You, sit down.

JASON. But I don't want –

(**MATTHEW** *puts the ice back on* **JASON***'s eye, which he's taken off.*)

BRENDA. Sweetie.

MATTHEW. If he doesn't want one, then he doesn't have to have one.

BRENDA. Great example you're setting.

ROBERT. Brenda just listen to me. Alright. No one knows. No one, outside of this room knows. Except for the boys who did it and they're not going to tell.

BRENDA. Which is why I'm calling the school.

ROBERT. It will get out.

BRENDA. So?

ROBERT. That Jason's been getting into fights.

BRENDA. He has not been getting into fights.

ROBERT. He kicked a boy in the groin.

BRENDA. To escape. In self-defense. They punched him.

Him.

ROBERT. No one will pay attention to that. They'll assume – he kicked a boy. Listen to me, Brenda.

BRENDA. This is insane. Insane. Someone attacked him.

JASON. Are you mad at me?

BRENDA. I'm not mad at you. Jason. Go upstairs please. I'll be up in a minute.

(*JASON looks to* **MATTHEW.** **MATTHEW** *nods.* **JASON** *goes upstairs.*)

ROBERT. We have to think about this carefully.

BRENDA. They hurt my son.

ROBERT. I know. Look, this was just because of Matthew. But what would happen if they think Jason is a risk too. Then it won't just be a couple eleven year olds. It'll be some thirteen year olds. Looking for a reason to lash out.

BRENDA. That's crazy.

ROBERT. Think about the repercussions. At least until next week. Until the hearing. Brenda, if this gets out. One wrong word, one misunderstood printed word and it could make things harder than they already are.

BRENDA. And what. Okay. So then. What? Send him to school. Just tell him to go to school. Like nothing...

ROBERT. Yes.

BRENDA. What about his eye? He has a black eye in case you didn't notice. They...fuckers!

ROBERT. He has the weekend. By Monday the swelling will have gone down.

(*The phone rings in her hand – she hasn't put it down since she first picked it up. They all stare at it.*)

Maybe you shouldn't –

BRENDA. Hello?

(*pause*)

(She hangs up, but keeps holding the phone in her hand.)

(pause)

(It rings again. She yanks it from the wall, unplugged, continuing to hold the phone.

Pause, as they watch her.

Another phone is still ringing.

BRENDA *finds the ringing cordless phone. She manically tries to take off the back of the phone.)*

ROBERT. Brenda...

BRENDA. The batteries.

MATTHEW. Mom, just...

*(**BRENDA** throws the cordless across the room. It stops ringing.*

Faintly, a phone can be heard ringing upstairs. They all look up.)

(pause)

BRENDA. I can't do this. I'm calling his school. *(pulls out mobile phone)*

ROBERT. Brenda.

BRENDA. Shut up. Just...okay?

MATTHEW. Mom, maybe you should just wait.

BRENDA. You shut up too.

ROBERT. Brenda, I'm urging you –

BRENDA. Just shutup, okay? You're not my lawyer. You're his. So let me do what I need to do.

ROBERT. You're upset. You're not thinking clearly.

MATTHEW. Mom, he's right.

BRENDA. Don't you tell me what's right. Don't you dare tell me – this is all – do you even care? Matthew...do you even....*(starts to cry)*

ROBERT. Just wait it out, Brenda. While they're watching.

BRENDA. Them? It always about them, huh? Do you know

what? Do you want to know something, Robert? I
don't give a shit about them. CRAWLING OUTSIDE
MY HOUSE! Like hungry fucking ANIMALS. What
do they want, huh?

Tell me. What do I have to give them to go away?
Another black eye? What?

JASON. *(off)* Mom?

MATTHEW. Maybe you should go to Jason, Mom.

BRENDA. I don't see you anywhere! I don't see you in any
of these pictures. Huh? No they don't want you. Can't
have you! Just the mother right? The real criminal.

JASON. *(off)* Mom?

MATTHEW. Mom, Jason's –

(Suddenly, **BRENDA** *heads for the front door.)*

ROBERT. Brenda.

BRENDA. Don't touch me. I said don't touch me!

JASON. *(off)* Mom! The bath's ready!

ROBERT. Brenda, don't do this.

BRENDA. What? Do what? Show my face. What? Show
them that I've got bags under my eyes? Huh? What
shouldn't they see? This is what they want isn't it!

ROBERT. Brenda!

*(***BRENDA*** opens the front door.)*

(Cameras start flashing.)

BRENDA. What is it you all want?! Huh! Look. Snap your
pictures! Here I am! Here she is. Brenda Kapowitz!
And look, I've got a birthmark on my right leg. And
I've got a capped tooth here. Look! Come and see!
(tears off her robe, stands naked) Here she is! Brenda
Kapowitz! The mother of the rapist!

*(The lights in the house go down, so that all can
be seen are the flashes of cameras against the
silhouette of* **BRENDA.** *The loud sound of the
cameras and crowd almost become slow motion
and distant except for the loud, amplified sound*

of a camera shutter and flash taking the pictures.

For a moment, it almost looks as if she is an icon/ celebrity posing for a press shoot.)

(blackout)

ACT 2

Scene One
Tuesday

(Three days later.

Three a.m. Living Room.

Six Hanukkah candles [shamash plus five] burn low. A freshly-opened bottle of wine and wine glass sit on the coffee table.

BRENDA *looks worse for wear. She is un-showered, her hair greasy and limp, no make-up.*

One of the blueprints of the mall is taped up to the wall. **BRENDA** *stands in front of it, staring at it, her back to us, a marker in her hand.*

Stillness. Quiet.

She steps back, tries to see it from a different angle.

After a long moment, she approaches it and draws a small stick figure in the centre of the mall. Observes. She's temporarily satisfied.

She catches sight of the bookcase – remembers...She takes out the video tape she hid behind the books in Act 1, scene 4.

She moves to the couch. Hesitates. Pours herself a glass of wine.

Turns on the TV. Puts the tape in the VHS player.

Play.

Sound starts of a News recording.

Voice of TV Reporter: "Brenda KaPOWitz, seen here –"

BRENDA *pauses it, watching her own face on the screen.*

Rewinds it. Play.

"Brenda KaPOWitz, seen here –"

Pauses it.

Rewinds it. Play.

"Brenda KaPOWitz, seen here –"

Pauses it.

She stares at it.

Long pause.

She turns off the TV. Continues staring at the blank screen.)

(fade out)

Scene Two

(Kitchen. Mid-afternoon.

The kitchen is no longer the perfectly clean room it was at the beginning of the play. Dirty dishes are piled beside the sink. A pile of the morning's papers sit on the counter.

BRENDA *sits at the kitchen table cutting and gluing pictures. She looks unkempt as she did in the last scene.*

The radio is on – a Christmas song finishes.

DJ. We're getting in the Christmas spirit here at Chum FM. After the ad break we'll get a bit more serious with a story from Belfast, Northern Ireland as they approach their first Christmas since the signing of the Good Friday Agreement earlier this year. And we'll also have an update on the Y2K bug.

Sounds from outside start growing. **BRENDA** *turns off the radio.*

MATTHEW *enters the side door. Flash. Reporters. Questions.*

He shuts the door hard behind him.

He and **BRENDA** *look at each other for a long moment.* **MATTHEW** *quickly grabs a carton of juice from the fridge and exits to the living room.*

The side door opens again. **ROBERT** *enters – flash, flash – shutting the door quickly behind him. It doesn't stop the sound of one reporter's voice saying "Where is Ms. Ka-POW-itz" squeezing through before the door closes, and hanging in the air.*

Long pause.

ROBERT *looks for a glass in the cupboard. Can't find one. Grabs a dirty one from the counter, washes it, and fills with water. Drinks.)*

ROBERT. Brenda. I think you / should

BRENDA. / I don't want to hear it.

ROBERT. You should talk to him.

BRENDA. That's what I pay you to do.

ROBERT. Brenda, he needs –

BRENDA. Don't tell me what he needs. He's my son.

ROBERT. Then you know that he's / probably

BRENDA. / You go talk to him then. Want to lend a listening ear. You have my blessing.

ROBERT. I think...Brenda, right now he needs his mother.

BRENDA. I'd say he needs a better lawyer.

ROBERT. He needed you there today.

BRENDA. What for? Photo ops?

ROBERT. He wanted you there.

BRENDA. Did he tell you that?

ROBERT. He didn't have to.

BRENDA. Well, we don't always get what we want.

ROBERT. Do you know what he looked like walking in there with no parent?

BRENDA. Like an adult, I presume.

(pause)

ROBERT. You can't stay in here forever, Brenda.

BRENDA. I don't see what bearing that has on my son's case.

ROBERT. I'm here as a friend, Brenda.

BRENDA. Well I'm paying you as a lawyer. I don't need friends.

ROBERT. Well as a lawyer, listen to me. He will be sentenced – as an adult – he will be sentenced at ten a.m. on Thursday. He needs you there.

(pause)

*(**ROBERT** exits to the living room.*

*
BRENDA stands for a moment in the kitchen.*

Goes to the fridge. Opens it. Stares into it. Mostly

empty. Shuts it.

Her mobile rings. She looks at the number. Answers.)

BRENDA. Hi Mom...

(Long pause as she listens to the other end. She lets her hand drop from her ear. We can hear the muffled voice on the other end angrily still talking. **BRENDA** *shuts her phone.*

The mobile phone begins to ring again. She presses a button, silencing it.

She lifts the next newspaper off the pile. Peruses it. Begins cutting out an article [about her].

ROBERT *enters. Watches her for a moment. She doesn't care.)*

ROBERT. I'll be here at nine a.m. on Thursday, to take him.

(beat)

Be sure to lock the door after me, won't you?

(beat)

I've increased the team outside. You'll still have Jimmy most days this week plus three others. And we're still looking into the digital security.

BRENDA. It was me.

I sent the photo – the Hanukkah one. Jason didn't print it. No one hacked into my computer. It was me.

I emailed it. Anonymously. But it was me. Modern world huh? Who needs the paparazzi?

ROBERT. I don't believe that. You wouldn't have done that.

BRENDA. Case closed. See that's what happens when you try to help them. You just fuck them up more. You should go. Don't want to catch something.

*(***ROBERT*** exits through the side kitchen door.*

A moment later, there's a knock at the side door. **BRENDA** *doesn't move.*

Knocking. More persistent.

BRENDA *gets up.)*

BRENDA. *(as she opens the door, thinking it's going to be Robert)* What is it?

(STEVEN stands on the other side.

Flash. Flash.)

STEVEN. Hey.

(pause)

(blackout)

Scene Three

(Kitchen. Late afternoon.

STEVEN *sits at the kitchen table, watching* **BRENDA** *make coffee.)*

BRENDA. Milk?

STEVEN. You know the answer to that.

BRENDA. No. I don't. Milk?

STEVEN. Yes. Please.

(She opens the fridge, gets milk.)

BRENDA. Don't look in my fridge.

STEVEN. What?

BRENDA. You were looking in my fridge. Examining.

STEVEN. It was open.

BRENDA. It's personal. Someone's fridge.

STEVEN. Your fridge.

BRENDA. It's personal.

STEVEN. You can tell a lot from sliced turkey and mustard.

BRENDA. Don't make fun of me please.

STEVEN. I'm not. You can. You're right. Put a whole life together based on the contents of someone's grocery cart, someone's fridge.

(sips)

It's good. Starbucks?

BRENDA. No.

STEVEN. Tastes like Starbucks.

(beat)

It's cozy.

BRENDA. You're saying it's small.

STEVEN. I didn't say that. It's warm. Snug.

BRENDA. The heater's on.

(They drink in silence for a few moments.)

STEVEN. I like the...wallpaper. From the last people? Or...?

BRENDA. Yeah. The last people.

STEVEN. Well, it's nice anyhow.

BRENDA. How'd you get the address?

STEVEN. What?

BRENDA. To the house.

STEVEN. Oh. It said somewhere. The street name.

BRENDA. Did it? The street name. Where'd it say?

STEVEN. No. Wait. Maybe not. Maybe just said the area. Yeah. Think it said Leslie and York Mills.

BRENDA. So how'd you know what street?

STEVEN. I looked it up.

BRENDA. What do you mean you looked it up?

STEVEN. You know. Like the Yellow Pages?

BRENDA. You looked us up in the Yellow Pages?

STEVEN. Yeah.

(pause)

BRENDA. We're not listed.

(pause)

STEVEN. I drove around. Just around the area. Only took me an hour.

BRENDA. How'd you know it was this house?

STEVEN. The CBC van out front kind of gave it away.

(He smiles. She smiles to herself.)

BRENDA. We are listed. By the way.

(beat)

You could have called. To ask the address. Would have been easier.

STEVEN. Would you have given it to me?

BRENDA. No. Probably not. *(beat)* They get a picture of you?

STEVEN. More than a few.

BRENDA. Expect to see yourself all over the city tomorrow morning.

STEVEN. It's fine. I flexed for them.

BRENDA. It's not funny.

STEVEN. Then why are you smiling?

BRENDA. I shouldn't be.

STEVEN. It's good to see you.

(*pause*)

(**STEVEN** *picks up one of the papers on the table.*)

Who's that foxy lady?

BRENDA. Stop.

STEVEN. I'd let her be the mother of my children.

BRENDA. Seriously. Stop. It's not funny.

(*pause*)

(**STEVEN** *pulls out some cigarettes. Offers her.*)

No.

STEVEN. Good for you.

BRENDA. You can't smoke in here.

(*He puts them away.*)

STEVEN. So how's work? You still at Pillars?

BRENDA. Why did you come here?

STEVEN. To talk.

BRENDA. I mean Toronto. The timing. A coincidence? You didn't fly all the way here to talk.

STEVEN. Maybe I came to see my family.

(*pause*)

BRENDA. I read an article recently. A couple of months ago, anyway. About how Winnipeg was now up and coming. Booming.

STEVEN. Yeah.

BRENDA. Must be good then. For business. If it's booming. You still ski?

STEVEN. What?

BRENDA. Wondered if you still did. Must be good out there.

STEVEN. Yeah. I do. *(short pause)* Do you?

BRENDA. No.

STEVEN. ...

    Where's Matthew?

BRENDA. Upstairs. *(pause)* Do you want me to call him down?

STEVEN. No. No. And Jason? Is he at school? What time does he usually get back?

BRENDA. ...

    Why are you here, Steven?

STEVEN. Business.

BRENDA. No, my house. What are you doing here?

    (pause)

STEVEN. I want to help.

BRENDA. There's not really anything left to help with.

    (pause)

STEVEN. Why don't I pick up Jason from school?

BRENDA. He gets a bus.

STEVEN. Okay. But today I'll pick him up.

BRENDA. He won't know who you are.

STEVEN. He knows who I am, Brenda.

BRENDA. He gets a bus from school, Steven.

STEVEN. Brenda. Come on, I just want to see my son.

BRENDA. Sons. You have two, remember.

    (silence)

STEVEN. Let's all have dinner together. It'll be fun.

BRENDA. Fun?

STEVEN. It's a start.

BRENDA. Of what?

    You go off again, what, in a week?

STEVEN. I won't be leaving in a week.

BRENDA. Two?

STEVEN. No. Brenda. I live here now. *(pause)* I moved

down here two months ago. For work.

BRENDA. You've been here. In Toronto. For two months.

STEVEN. I'm living at Yonge and Eglinton.

BRENDA. Two months.

STEVEN. I wanted to wait until I was more settled in.

BRENDA. You've got great timing.

STEVEN. And then I read about...

BRENDA. Two months.

STEVEN. I'm sorry. I should've, should've come before. But I...well, what can I say. But I'm here now, Brenda.

BRENDA. Yes. You sure are. *(beat)* What is this, Steven?

STEVEN. I want to help.

BRENDA. You haven't been too bothered about doing that the last five years.

STEVEN. Yes we know that, Brenda. But I want to now. I'm here.

BRENDA. We've established that. Here you are.

STEVEN. I just want to help.

BRENDA. And what is it you can help with? Legal fees – what?

STEVEN. No. That's not what I...I mean I can. Of course I can do that too. If that's what you need.

BRENDA. No. I don't want your money.

STEVEN. Of course.

BRENDA. So then what? What is it you want to help with?

STEVEN. I want to be a father.

(Pause. She starts laughing.)

BRENDA. Oh. That's classic. You want to be a father. You've been watching too much television.

STEVEN. I feel like...when I read about...I just keep thinking what if...what if...you know?

BRENDA. No. I don't.

STEVEN. I feel like...this is my fault.

BRENDA. What?

STEVEN. What he did. I feel like it's my fault. If I...if I had been there, I could've – he wouldn't have...

BRENDA. What? He wouldn't have raped some girl? He wouldn't have raped three girls?

STEVEN. If he'd had a father, to, to, to –

BRENDA. To what?

STEVEN. To teach him. If I'd been there to teach him about women.

BRENDA. Excuse me?

STEVEN. I move across the country. Just leaving you with two boys.

STEVEN. He had no one to show him respect for women. I mean what kind of example had I been?

BRENDA. I showed him how to respect women!

STEVEN. I'm saying this is my fault! You did as much as you could, I know you did. A single mother. That's why I'm saying if I'd been there –

BRENDA. But not enough. I did as much as I could, but it wasn't enough. That's what you're saying.

STEVEN. That's not what I'm saying.

BRENDA. If he'd had a man in his life then this wouldn't have happened.

STEVEN. Well don't you think so?

BRENDA. Fuck you. Fuck you, Steven.

STEVEN. Brenda. I'm taking the blame here.

BRENDA. You need to leave, Steven.

STEVEN. Brenda –

BRENDA. You need to leave. Jason will be home soon. I don't want you here when he gets home.

STEVEN. Brenda, let me take responsibility for this. Let me make this right.

BRENDA. Your taking responsibility is saying I did something wrong.

STEVEN. No.

BRENDA. I wasn't enough. I missed out on teaching him something. If you'd been here –

STEVEN. Well, think about if I had.

BRENDA. Get out.

STEVEN. Why are you so stubborn?! Why won't you let me do this?

BRENDA. Do what?

STEVEN. Make things right. Or at least better.

BRENDA. Alright. Tell me. Tell me Steven how you plan to make things right.

(silence)

Well?

(She calms down.)

Well?

STEVEN. I don't think it's a good idea for Jason to be around Matthew. Under the circumstances. We don't – you don't want him influencing him. So I thought...well at least until the sentencing, at least while Matthew's here, Jason should, for the rest of the week at least... come live with me.

*(**BRENDA** stares at him. Let's out a small horrifying laugh.)*

BRENDA. You think...you actually think I'm going to give my child to you?

STEVEN. He's our child, Brenda.

BRENDA. As I recall you have no custodial rights over him. As I recall you gave those up.

STEVEN. Which is why I'm asking, Brenda. Let me help you.

BRENDA. By taking my son away?

STEVEN. I'm not taking him away. Brenda, do you want this to happen again?

BRENDA. You're something else, Steven. You really are.

STEVEN. You think it's good for a seven year-old to be

around him, around Matthew?

BRENDA. He's eight.

STEVEN. I couldn't live with myself if the same thing happened to Jason.

BRENDA. Steven. You need to leave.

STEVEN. Think about this rationally.

BRENDA. Now.

STEVEN. Brenda think about what's best for your son.

BRENDA. I have thought about what's best for my son his whole life!

STEVEN. So then let him come with me. At least while Matthew's here.

BRENDA. Get the fuck out, Steven.

STEVEN. I don't want to get lawyers involved. But I will. If I have to. To protect my son.

BRENDA. You have no rights over – how dare you even –

(**STEVEN** *holds up the newspaper with the naked picture of* **BRENDA** *on the front.*)

(**BRENDA** *gasps like she's been punched. Can't believe he'd stoop that low.*)

STEVEN. I just want to protect them.

(*Long Pause.* **BRENDA** *begins preparing seven candles in the menorah [six plus shamash]. She doesn't light them.*)

BRENDA. Do you remember that ball, the yellow and pink one, he wouldn't ever let go of? Stripes. Or was it polka-dots? Carried it with him everywhere – for a week it probably was. Do you remember?

Matthew was four, five maybe. And his face, you could just see. And you were sitting, probably where you are now. But in another kitchen. And I was...and I could just see in his face. Before he said anything, before he even

And you said we shouldn't tell them. They'd never know it was his ball. We couldn't afford to replace anything

of our own, never mind the neighbors' window. But I
wouldn't let you.

Made you walk over with him, apologize.

(pause)

Maybe they shouldn't be in the same house. While all
this...You look me in the eye and you tell me that you
really mean it, that you really want to be a father.

STEVEN. Brenda. I do.

BRENDA. Alright. You want your son to live with you? You
want to be a father? Who am I to say no to that.

STEVEN. Do you mean that?

BRENDA. ...Yes. I do.

STEVEN. Brenda. Thank you.

BRENDA. Do you want to take him now?

STEVEN. I thought he was at school.

BRENDA. Jason? He is.

You don't want them living in the same house, you
want to be a father? Then Matthew can come live with
you for the rest of the week.

STEVEN. Brenda, that's not what I –

BRENDA. You said you wanted to be a father, now's your
turn.

Matthew! Come down stairs please!

(at STEVEN) Your father's here.

(blackout)

Scene Four

(Kitchen. Evening.

BRENDA *clears the remnants of dinner – with only two place settings.*

Stillness.

The door from the living room opens. **MATTHEW** *stands in the doorway for a moment, hesitant. He enters carrying a plate with virtually untouched dinner on it.)*

MATTHEW. Jason wants to know if you're coming to light the candles.

BRENDA. No. You can light them every night but it won't come. In real life, the miracle doesn't come. What did he say?

MATTHEW. He just asked if you're –

BRENDA. No. Your father.

MATTHEW. He didn't say anything.

BRENDA. He didn't say anything.

(beat)

He said nothing. You just sat there in silence, did you? The two of you?

MATTHEW. We were standing actually.

(beat)

Said he didn't have anything to say to me.

(pause)

Why'd he come?

BRENDA. Didn't he tell you?

MATTHEW. I thought to see me.

BRENDA. No.

MATTHEW. Is he coming back?

BRENDA. Maybe. Probably. I don't know.

MATTHEW. So why'd he bother to come? Nothing to say.

Should've just...

BRENDA. Didn't come to see you. Be perfectly happy never to see you again.

MATTHEW. He wouldn't have come then.

BRENDA. No?

MATTHEW. Just came to see you then?

BRENDA. No. Not me either.

Came to see your brother. Wants to take him. Make sure he doesn't turn out like you.

MATTHEW. ...You're lying.

BRENDA. No.

MATTHEW. I don't believe you.

BRENDA. Don't. Won't change it.

You can believe what you want, but in the end it doesn't change it, the truth.

(beat)

MATTHEW. Jason must be happy then. If he's going to see Dad.

BRENDA. He's not.

And you're not going to tell him. You're not going to tell him that Steven was here. Yes? Matthew? You understand?

No one is taking Jason anywhere.

This I won't let you do.

MATTHEW. Me?

I don't get / what

BRENDA. / You don't get it? He can get straight A's, get into Schulich, but he doesn't get it.

MATTHEW. ...

BRENDA. I'll break it down for you. You may have destroyed yourself. You may have destroyed me. But I won't let it affect Jason, this...this thing you've created. This cloud, this monster that's engulfing this house. I won't let you make him a part of it.

MATTHEW. You know I never meant –

BRENDA. I don't care what you meant, Matthew. I am done caring, Matthew. There's nothing left. No more caring. No more sympathy. Or empathy. Or even the slightest emotion. Look at me. All there is is this. Empty flesh. It's all hollow now. And all that's left is her *(picks up a newspaper photo of herself)* And her *(another)*. And her *(another)*. You are what I have created. And this is what you've created. All that's left for you is an empty void. And if you find anything, the slightest bit of emotion, I'll tell you what you'll find. Hate. You have raped me of everything else. And that's all that's left now. All I have left to give you. Hate. I can barely see you. But I can see clearly you're not a child. Not my child.

So if something happens to Jason because of you. If he takes him because of you...so help me God, Matthew. So help me God.

(Long pause.

MATTHEW *exits to the living room.* BRENDA *remains still. Staring at the spot where he was.*

She scrapes the food from Matthew's plate into the garbage. Then instead of putting in the dishwasher, she just drops the whole plate in the garbage can.)

(blackout)

Transition

(News programme.)

MALE DJ. On grounds of perjury to a grand jury and obstruction of justice.

FEMALE DJ. But Clinton was *not* impeached on other charges including abuse of power, meaning –

MALE DJ. Lewinsky got on her knees of her own accord.

FEMALE DJ. Oh Frankie.

MALE DJ. *(laughing)* What? It's not me saying that, it's the American House of Representatives. Which maybe segues into our next bit of news: It's been a mere 8 months since the release of the little pill that could – Viagra. And year end forecasts show sales through the roof.

FEMALE DJ. And you would know Frankie.

MALE DJ. Trust me, I don't need it...

(They laugh. Their laughs echoing into:)

Scene Five
Wednesday

(**MATTHEW**'s *Bedroom. 6 a.m.*

MATTHEW's *asleep in bed.* **JASON** *is pointing his camera at* **MATTHEW**. *He snaps a photo. He puts the camera in his pocket.*

He starts looking through the closet. **MATTHEW** *wakes up.)*

MATTHEW. What are you doing?

JASON. Just looking.

MATTHEW. You shouldn't go through people's things.

JASON. I was just looking.

MATTHEW. What are you looking for?

JASON. Nothing. Just looking.

MATTHEW. Well, you shouldn't. Get you into trouble.

JASON. Like you did?

(silence)

Are you going to be here when I get home?

MATTHEW. Where else would I be?

JASON. So you're an adult now. Does that mean you can do what you want?

MATTHEW. What?

JASON. Heard mom say. They've decided you're an adult.

(pause)

Can I have your room?

MATTHEW. What's wrong with yours?

JASON. I just like yours. Can I?

MATTHEW. I don't know. You're moving anyhow.

JASON. But until then.

MATTHEW. Ask Mom.

(pause)

Aren't you late for school?

JASON. No way. It's not even seven. Mom's not even up yet. Can you help me with something?

MATTHEW. What?

JASON. Hold on.

(*JASON rushes out of the room.*

MATTHEW sits up. He peers through the blinds.

JASON reenters with some homework papers.)

How much longer do you think they'll stay for?

(beat)

MATTHEW. What's that?

JASON. Book report. Guided Reading Questions.

MATTHEW. You haven't done any of them.

JASON. I don't know the answers.

MATTHEW. Did you read the book? You have to read the book, Jason.

JASON. I did. I just can't remember the answers. Can you help me?

MATTHEW. I haven't read the book.

JASON. Please.

MATTHEW. I haven't read the book, Jason. I don't know the answers. When's it due?

JASON. Today.

MATTHEW. You shouldn't leave things to the last minute.

JASON. I don't. Never mind. It doesn't matter. *(goes to closet)*

MATTHEW. Would you get out of there?

JASON. I'm just looking. *(takes hoodie with the holes in it)* Can I have this? *(starts to put it on)*

MATTHEW. It's too big on you.

JASON. No it's not. Please.

MATTHEW. Yeah. Fine.

JASON. Sick.

> (**MATTHEW** *begins doing bicep curls with hand-weights.*)

> Why do you do that? Matthew?

MATTHEW. Makes you stronger.

JASON. Can I try?

MATTHEW. What do I care?

> (**JASON** *picks up a smaller hand-weight, uses two hands.*)

JASON. This is tiring.

MATTHEW. That's the point.

> (*beat*)

JASON. Was Dad here?

MATTHEW. ...

JASON. Was he?

MATTHEW. Who told you that?

JASON. Heard Mom say.

MATTHEW. Shouldn't eavesdrop. It's rude.

JASON. Wasn't. Just heard, that's all. Can't help it if I hear it.

> (*pause*)

> Was he?

MATTHEW. Yeah.

JASON. Oh. Is he coming back?

MATTHEW.

JASON. Matthew?

MATTHEW. No.

JASON. What did he come for?
Matthew?

MATTHEW. I don't know okay.

JASON. Did he bring us presents?

MATTHEW. No.

> (**MATTHEW***'s curls get visibly faster. Pause.*)

JASON. I'll bring you presents. Try to at least. When I come visit you.

(**MATTHEW** *stops doing the bicep curls.*)

If you tell me what you want, I'll bring it. We can write letters and stuff.

MATTHEW. ...

JASON. Can I bring friends with me? Can I bring Brandon with me sometimes? And we can even bake you cookies or something, maybe. Right, Matthew?

(**MATTHEW** *suddenly starts to cry.*)

Matthew?

(*JASON is unsure what to do. So just watches him.*)

Should I get Mom?

(*Pause.* **MATTHEW**'s *crying subsides.*

JASON *takes out an open packet of gummy bears from his pocket*)

Here.

MATTHEW. Shouldn't eat them so early in the day.

JASON. We can just have one.

(*hands* **MATTHEW** *one*)

Do you want a different colour?

(**MATTHEW** *shakes his head, pops it in his mouth.*)

I like to eat the head first.

(*JASON bites the head. Then makes scary noises while he moves the headless bear toward* **MATTHEW.**)

Ahhh!

(**MATTHEW** *gives a small smile. Then takes hold of* **JASON**'s *face.*)

MATTHEW. Your eye looks better.

JASON. Yeah. It doesn't hurt. Never really did. Do you want another one?

MATTHEW. No. Thanks. (*beat*) I'm going to take a shower. You should do your book report.

*(***MATTHEW** *exits.*

JASON *eats another gummy bear.*

He admires himself in the mirror.

He picks up some hair gel from the dresser. Applies some to his hair and spikes it up in a faux-hawk, like **MATTHEW***'s hair.)*

(fade out)

Scene Six

(Kitchen. Morning.

Cereal is prepared for **JASON** *on the kitchen table.*
BRENDA *is on the phone.)*

BRENDA. I just don't know how many more times I can change it. We can iron out the details once there's a structure...

(**JASON** *enters. Sits down and begins eating his cereal.)*

...Then let me speak to the board directly...of course you can...just try, alright. I'll speak to you later.

(**JASON** *stands up and gets some sugar. Starts spooning it over his cereal. It's only now that* **BRENDA** *really notices him.*

She takes the sugar while he's still pouring.)

What are you doing?

JASON. It tastes like shit.

BRENDA. Excuse me?

JASON. ...

BRENDA. What did you say?

JASON. Nothing.

BRENDA. Better have been nothing. You watch your mouth, Jason.

JASON. I just like it better with sugar.

BRENDA. Well it's not good for you. You'll concentrate better without the sugar.

JASON. Is Dad coming back?

Mom?

BRENDA. I don't know what you mean.

JASON. He was here yesterday. So is he coming back?

BRENDA. Is that what Matthew told you?

JASON. Is he?

BRENDA. No.

JASON. How come?

BRENDA. Because he's not.

JASON. Doesn't he want to see me?

Mom, I'm asking you a question.

BRENDA. And I've answered it. He's not coming back.

JASON. Then why did he come in the first place?

BRENDA. Eat yours cereal before it gets...just eat your cereal.

JASON. But Mom.

BRENDA. Why...why is your hair wet?

JASON. It's not.

(**BRENDA** *approaches and touches it.*)

BRENDA. What's in your hair? Where did you – why is there gel in / your

JASON. / I like it.

BRENDA. Since when do you wear gel?

JASON. Since today.

BRENDA. Well, I don't think you're allowed to have gel in your hair at school. Go wash it out please.

JASON. I'm keeping it in.

BRENDA. It looks ridiculous.

JASON. No it doesn't.

BRENDA. Yes. It does. Eight year-olds don't wear gel in their hair.

JASON. Matthew does.

(*beat*)

BRENDA. Well, you're not your brother. And he's not eight. He's...this isn't a choice, Jason.

(**JASON** *pulls the hood over his head and continues to eat with his head down.*)

Where did you get...that sweatshirt's not yours.

JASON. Yes it is.

BRENDA. No it's / not.

JASON. / Matthew gave it to me.

(pause)

BRENDA. I've told you about going through other people's things.

JASON. He gave it to me.

BRENDA. You need to put it back.

JASON. I told you he gave it to me!

BRENDA. Don't raise your voice at me, Jason. You don't speak / to your

JASON. / Well I've told you a million times, he gave it to me.

Today's Matthew's last day, right?

BRENDA. You can't – what?

JASON. It is, right?

(Beat. She nods.)

So can I stay home with him then?

BRENDA. No.

JASON. But I want –

BRENDA. No, Jason. You asked me a question. I gave you an answer. And it's no. If anyone bothers you, you tell your teacher, alright. Take your hood off please. It's not very polite when you're inside.

JASON. It's cause you weren't a good Mom that he's going to jail.

BRENDA. ...Where did you...who said that to you, Jason? Jason. Where did you – I'm asking you a question, Jason.

JASON. ...

BRENDA. Jason, you answer me when I ask you a question.

And I asked you to *(She pulls the hood off his head.)* take this hood off. You don't say things like that to me, alright? I...I did the...you just, you just don't say things like that to me, alright?

(She takes the cereal bowl from in front of him.)

Go get changed.

JASON. I wasn't finished that!

BRENDA. You have to go. Go get changed.

*(***JASON*** doesn't move.)*

Take that stupid sweatshirt off and then – and wash out your hair – and you have to go. I put clothes for you to wear on the end of your bed.

JASON. I'm wearing this.

BRENDA. Jason – I won't – take it off. Now.

Jason.

(He stares at her contemptuously and doesn't move from the chair.)

For God's sake.

(She goes to him, lifts him off the chair, and struggles to get the hoodie off him.)

JASON. No...Mom!...Mom, no!

(She gets the sweatshirt off him.)

BRENDA. Go put on the sweater I prepared for you.

JASON. You're a cold bitch.

(Without hesitation, **BRENDA** *slaps him across the face.*

A very brief moment, as they stand close to one another, staring, before:

JASON *starts crying/screaming and runs out of the room.)*

(long pause)

*(***BRENDA*** lifts the sweatshirt up to her face. Smells it. Almost hugs it.*

She hesitates a moment, unsure of what to do with it. Then she quickly stuffs it in the garbage can. Closes the lid, and sits on it.

Loud music suddenly comes from upstairs.)

(fade to black)

Scene Seven

Living Room. Afternoon.

The sound of keys in the door. Noise of press out-side.

TESS *enters, with bags, locking the door behind her.*

She hangs up her coat.

Looks around for a moment.

She goes to the laundry room, and keeps coming out with various cleaning supplies, which she sets down in the living room.

She turns on the radio – "I Want You Back" by *NSYNC.

She takes a pile of newspapers from the coffee table, and puts them in a garbage bag.

She starts dusting the bookcase.

BRENDA *enters down the stairs.*

BRENDA. Tess. Sorry. I didn't know –

TESS. Hello Brenda.

(She lowers the music)

Sorry. I didn't hear what you said.

BRENDA. Just I didn't...didn't think you'd be coming today.

TESS. What do you mean? Second Wednesday.

BRENDA. Well, yes, of course, just / with

TESS. / Almost Christmas.

BRENDA. Yes. It is.

TESS. I brought you something for Hanukkah. My friend told me what to get.

TESS *retrieves a box of Matzah. Gives it to* BRENDA.

TESS. For you all to enjoy.

BRENDA. ... *(hesitates, stops herself.)*

Tess...listen...sorry I should've... You can go home. I'll still pay you. Sorry I should've –

TESS. Why?

BRENDA. It's just that –

TESS. No. No. This place needs a clean.

BRENDA. Yes. It does. It's just...we're...I'm

TESS. No need to explain. I stay out of the way.

She smiles and keeps cleaning. Brenda goes to the window. Looks out.

TESS. So many of them, eh?

BRENDA. Yes.

TESS. Don't you worry, Brenda. Soon they'll be gone. Home to their families, yes.

BRENDA. How are your kids?

TESS. Big. Always getting bigger.

BRENDA. They tend to do that.

TESS. Timothy, my little one you know, he is getting a big mouth. I tell him if he doesn't learn to shut it, someone will do it for him when he is older, right?

All the time on the subway everyone is looking. So cute. He is so cute, such a good little boy. Ha. He is a monster. I want to tell them he is not so cute when he is running around the house like the Tazmanian devil.

BRENDA. And how's...uh...

TESS. Eric is fine. He likes hockey. Like your son, right? Fast game. Too violent for me. Bam, bam, bam, bam. Always getting hurt. But it helps them, they say, helps the brain to move. To think fast, right. So maybe they will grow up smart. Strong and smart. That is what I want.

But you know they are always fighting. I tell them they should be friends, right. I even told them I remember your boys, Jason and Matthew they never fight. Never when I am over did they ever fight.

BRENDA. They did sometimes.

TESS. My boys. All the time. Maybe I'll give them to you. You know what to do. Better than me. Maybe I'll give them to you. *(laughs)*

And Fernando he is a good dad, sometimes. Maybe I'll give him to you with the kids. (laughs). Maybe I'll send them with you to Halifax. I'm going to miss this house. Always the same where the dust is hiding. You know. No tricks. No surprises. All ready to move?

BRENDA. No. No.

TESS. Need to start packing. Pack, pack, pack, pack. When do they move in? The new people? Maybe they'll hire me. *(laughs)*

BRENDA. Do you mind if I turn this off?

TESS. No problem. I have a discman. Fernando get it for me. Early Christmas present. Has Shockwave, whatever that does.

BRENDA. There were...Tess, did you see...there were papers on here.

TESS. Yes, old ones.

BRENDA. Where are they?

TESS. Garbage.

BRENDA. They're not...they're not garbage.

TESS *stops her from taking them out of the garbage.*

TESS. Brenda. They're garbage.

BRENDA *understands* TESS's *meaning.*

TESS *puts on her headphones/music; sweeps the floor.* BRENDA *sits on the couch. Though she knows*

TESS *can't hear her, she proceeds to speak.*

BRENDA I uh...I went to the grocery store. And it's only as she's paying. In front of me, that I notice. Same for her. Only then that she...and it took a second to, I knew right away I knew the face but took a few seconds to place it, put it with...and by then it's too late to look away, right?

She had quite a lot. Bananas and Tomatoes and coffee. Fairtrade. And how alike we might have been. I thought we might have been friends even. In some other...if you were looking at us, you might have even thought we were friends. Old friends. If my son hadn't raped her daughter.

I think she was maybe going to say something. Her lip, it started to, ever so slowly but I looked away. Concentrated hard on the fair-trade sticker. And I wanted...just for a second. To switch. Feel what it was like. To be her. This woman. And for her to be me.

It was the young woman's voice that snapped me out of it. I don't think she knew. By the way she. She bagged everything. For me. And then wouldn't you know it, it's always the way isn't it, it's to be – her car was next to mine. Not even – it was directly next to mine. What could I do? Where could I hide? And I thought, I have nothing to hide from. I have done nothing wrong. And when she saw me, she...I was ready, armor out, when she said...she said... "I'm sorry"...and then she, or maybe it was me, she took my hand. Held it just for a second, but it felt like, or maybe it was...

I've lost him, Tess. She lost a part of her daughter that night, and I lost a part of my son. Hold on as tight as you like but one way or another they slip away. All you can do is standby. Watch them fly, or watch them fall, but be there. Standing by.

TESS *begins to vacuum in front of the couch where* **BRENDA** *sits.*

Fade out.

Scene Eight
Thursday

(Kitchen. Morning.

STEVEN *is in the kitchen. He paces.*

He opens the window a little bit, and then lights a cigarette and smokes out the window.

The sound of someone coming.

He throws the cigarette out the window and quickly closes the window.

BRENDA *enters. She is showered, made-up, together.*

She hands **STEVEN** *a small overnight bag.)*

BRENDA. Clothes for tomorrow. Pyjamas, toothbrush, toothpaste, slippers –

STEVEN. – I have toothpaste, Brenda.

BRENDA. And make sure he really brushes. That he actually puts the toothpaste on the brush and doesn't just pretend. Do it for him to make sure. And if he can't sleep or wants to come home, call me right away.

STEVEN. You said he was excited.

BRENDA. He is. Just if –

STEVEN. He'll be fine Brenda.

(She turns away. Pours some coffee.)

BRENDA. You made coffee.

STEVEN. Something to do. *(smiles)*

Thank you, Brenda. For understanding.

BRENDA. It's one night.

STEVEN. I know I haven't exactly been –

BRENDA. I'm not doing this for you. To be honest I couldn't care less about what you think. I'm doing this for Jason.

STEVEN. Still. Thank you. For listening.

BRENDA. It's not to do with anything you said.

STEVEN. Brenda, you don't have to –

BRENDA. I need you to know. It's not. Because I don't think you could've changed anything. I firmly believe that. But Jason wants to see you. And if I don't let him he'll find his own way to. Not now. But one day.

STEVEN. You'll be alright then? Tonight. By yourself in the house.

BRENDA. I've been alright for many years, Steven.

STEVEN. You could come over for dinner. The three of us together. See the house.

BRENDA. No. Thank you. I'll be fine.

(pause)

STEVEN. I'll see you tomorrow then. I'll have him at school for nine.

BRENDA. Be careful on the roads.

STEVEN. Forgot to say last time. Happy Hanukkah.

(He exits to outside. We hear the reporters as he does.

MATTHEW *enters with the empty plate from his dinner. He wears a suit.)*

BRENDA. Was it good?

(He nods.)

You look nice. Come here. Your tie.

MATTHEW. What?

(She straightens it.)

BRENDA. There.

MATTHEW. Robert here yet?

BRENDA. No. He'll meet you there.

MATTHEW. How am I –

BRENDA. I'm taking you.

Do you want some breakfast?

MATTHEW. No. Thanks.

How come? You're taking me? Thought you weren't leaving the house until...

BRENDA. Because you're my son.

(*pause*)

MATTHEW. Weird to think I'll never see this house again. You know?

BRENDA. You will. Probably.

I've put the move on hold.

MATTHEW. What about your mall?

BRENDA. I've done what I can. Be up to someone else to oversee the next stage of its development.

(*She gets the menorah from the counter. She's prepared it with all nine candles.*)

Come on. Better light these. Last day.

MATTHEW. You can't light them in the morning.

BRENDA. I can do what I want. Now come on. (*She lights the shamash.*)

You need to sing.

MATTHEW. Mom.

BRENDA. Please.

(*They begin to light the other candles.*)

MATTHEW. (*quietly, slowly, sings*) Barukh Atta Adonay Eloheynu Melekh Ha-olam

Asher (*he begins to cry*) Kiddeshanu Be-mitsvotav Ve-tsivanu

Lehadlik Ner

(*By now, **MATTHEW** is sobbing so hard he can't finish singing the prayer. All the candles are lit.*

BRENDA *puts her hand gently on his shoulder.*

MATTHEW *falls into her, begins sobbing into her chest. And then **BRENDA** starts to cry.*)

(*pause*)

BRENDA. Hey. Come on. You have to...you have to make a wish now and blow the candles out.

MATTHEW. You're not supposed to blow them out.

BRENDA. Let's do it anyway. Make a wish. Come on.

(They both close their eyes. Blow the candles out. A moment.

BRENDA *fixes* **MATTHEW***'s tie again.)*

We should get going.

(They put on their coats, hoods/hats.)

You ready?

*(***MATTHEW*** nods.*

BRENDA *holds out her hand.* **MATTHEW** *takes it.*

BRENDA *opens the door. Immediately the sound of reporters takes over, with the flash of cameras.*

They step out the door. Closing it behind them.)

(blackout)